STRANGE OBJECTS

STRANGE OBJECTS

Gary Crew

Simon & Schuster Books for Young Readers

Published by Simon & Schuster
New York   London   Toronto   Sydney   Tokyo   Singapore

SIMON & SCHUSTER BOOKS FOR YOUNG READERS
Simon & Schuster Building, Rockefeller Center, 1230 Avenue of the Americas,
New York, New York 10020. Copyright © 1990 by Gary Crew
Originally published in Australia in 1990 by
Reed International Books, Australia
First U.S. edition 1993
SIMON SCHUSTER BOOKS FOR YOUNG READERS is a trademark of
Simon & Schuster.
Designed by Paula R. Szafranski
The text of this book was set in Sabon.
Manufactured in the United States of America   10   9   8   7   6   5   4   3   2   1

Library of Congress Cataloging-in-Publication Data

Crew, Gary
       Strange objects / by Gary Crew.
          p.   cm.
       Summary: After discovering valuable relics from a seventeenth-century
    shipwreck, a sixteen-year-old Australian disappears under mysterious
    circumstances.
       [1. Mystery and detective stories.   2. Australia—Fiction.]
    I. Title.
    PZ7.C867St   1993   [Fic]—dc20   92-30519   CIP
    ISBN: 0-671-79759-X
    "Paradise by the Dashboard Light" by Jim Steinman (page 139),
    copyright © 1977 by Edward B. Marks Music Company. Used by
    permission. All rights reserved.

For there are strange objects in the great abyss,
and the seeker of dreams must take care not to stir up,
or meet, the wrong ones. . . .

—H. P. Lovecraft, *Dagon and Other Macabre Tales*

Notes on the Disappearance of Steven Messenger, Aged 16 Years

by Dr. Hope Michaels, Director, Western Australian Institute of Maritime Archaeology

On August 29, 1986, when sixteen-year-old Steven Messenger was reported missing from his mother's trailer unit at the Midway Roadhouse, an isolated truck stop on Highway One, Western Australia, local police treated his disappearance as a routine case of a short-term runaway, believing that he would probably return when his limited finances had been exhausted.

It was not until five days later, when I opened my mail at the Institute to find a series of documents supposedly written by Steven Messenger, that his disappearance attracted national attention. The reason for the sudden interest in the boy's fate was quite simple: in April 1986 Messenger had accidentally discovered certain highly valuable relics from a seventeenth-century shipwreck. Among these relics were an iron pot (which became commonly known as the "cannibal pot"), a leather-bound journal, and a mummified human hand.

An ongoing problem with Messenger's discoveries was that many authorities, including myself, considered that they were not all accounted for. Following a detailed examination of the mummified hand, it was established that a ring had been recently removed and that this object was most likely in the possession of Steven Messenger or one of the other teenagers who had been with him at the time of the discovery.

Although various appeals were made for the recovery of the ring, including a personal letter to Messenger, these achieved nothing—until the afternoon of Wednesday September 3, 1986. On that date I received in the mail a project book (neatly covered in newspaper*) and an accompanying note, which claimed that the contents were the work of Steven Messenger himself.

The project book was of the conventional pulp-paper type, with ninety-six pages, measuring 8½ by 11 inches. When the newspaper cover had been removed, the cardboard beneath showed a still from the 1977 George Lucas film *Star Wars*. The caption printed at the bottom right-hand corner read: "A lifepod lands on the barren surface of Tatooine."

Inside were pages covered in handwriting (black ballpoint pen, generally uniform and labeled "Messenger, Midway Roadhouse") or pasted-in press clippings and photocopied articles from books and magazines. Each item—whether handwritten or in print—was individually numbered and its source (newspaper, book, etc.) had been carefully recorded. Many of the larger newspaper articles were neatly folded to keep within the edges of the project book cover.

One item (marked "Item 3") was an audio cassette. This had been placed in an envelope that was pasted onto the page.

A perusal of the project book was enough to convince me of two things: first, that Messenger had written the material and, second, that the boy was seriously considering absconding from his home—or had already done so.

Consequently, I managed to contact his home address, the Midway Roadhouse. Only then did I learn that he had been missing for almost a week.

---

*The Hamelin Herald, Friday, August 29, 1986—Ed.

The resulting search for Steven Messenger is now in its second year. An inquiry into his disappearance (Hamelin, December 1986) proved inconclusive. Although there have been several unconfirmed sightings in the northwest (January 1987, Broome; and May 1988, the Kimberleys) the Western Australian police have no evidence of Messenger's whereabouts. He is also sought by the Commonwealth Police for breaches of the Historic Shipwrecks Act (1976) and, if convicted, would face severe fines and/or imprisonment.

Strange Objects is the first publication of the entire contents of the documents contained in the project book that Messenger mailed to the Institute in September 1986. Also included are extracts from the Messenger investigation and other evidence relevant to the case.

I trust that any reader who may have information on the whereabouts of Steven Messenger or of the historic ring will contact either myself or the police without hesitation.

Dr. Hope Michaels
Western Australian Institute of Maritime Archaeology

The
Messenger
Documents

Item 1

From the Evening Truth, *April 14, 1986*

Schoolboy Stirs Cannibal Pot
in Mutilation Mystery

Perth, Monday. Central CIB detectives are today continuing investigations into the weekend discovery of a human hand by a 16-year-old schoolboy.

Steven Messenger, a student at Hamelin High School, discovered the hand in a cave among cliffs to the north of the Murchison River mouth. The hand had been sealed in an iron kettle and hidden at the back of the cave in an area where Messenger and other students were spending the weekend on a marine biology field trip for their school.

Police and police cadets are searching the cave and nearby beach for further human remains. The hand is believed to be that of a child or teenager.

Interviewed at the site, Senior Sergeant Ronald Norman said that the investigation had top priority because the Murchison was attracting more tourists each year. "The isolation of the area means that backpackers and campers may be placing themselves at risk from visits by undesirables who are attracted to these out-of-the-way places," he said. "The wilderness region of the Murchison basin has a history of unexplained disappearances."

Messenger's discovery of the hand, which had been severed at the wrist, was the first evidence available to police that may be linked with these disappearances.

No connection has yet been made between the hand and the iron kettle in which it was found. Because of its shape, the kettle has become known on site as the "cannibal pot." Locals believe it could be of Malaysian origin, since it resembled those once used to prepare bêches-de-mer, or sea slugs, for sale as a delicacy in Southeast Asia.

Hamelin High biology teacher, Jock Ericson, who had been supervising the students, said yesterday, "I heard the kids calling out and dropped what I was doing. I thought someone was injured. After they had seen the hand it took me quite a while to settle them down. They were very upset."

An Education Department spokesperson said the children involved in the incident should be given special consideration by teachers over the next few days.

A man's leather wallet was also found in the cave.

Item 2

Messenger, Midway Roadhouse

I found the cannibal pot on the last night of a three-day biology field trip to the mouth of the Murchison River. That was a Saturday night and after supper, the teachers, Ericson, and a new woman called Schuler, had gone down the beach by themselves. I heard some kids say that this pair had a thing going for each other but no one followed them to find out for sure.

That afternoon the weather had turned bad, with squalls coming in from the sea, but under the overhang of the cliffs someone found enough dry driftwood to keep a fire going. I was sitting off to one side, watching, and even after midnight I could still see the others lying around on blankets, smoking, and poking sticks into the flames. I could hear their voices too, carried on the wind. They were telling horror stories.

There was a hitchhiker, a homicidal maniac who walked the highway at night waiting for victims. But if anyone stopped to pick him up—maybe a tourist, or even a truck driver—then days later that person's vehicle would be found abandoned and empty. And between the meat-ants' nests, beside the highway, a cop might find bits of clothing, maybe some buttons or a buckle or a zipper, but never a body, not so much as a single bone.

With the wind moaning up off the night sea the way it did, and the shadows from the flames moving among the rocks, I felt my skin crawl, and the goose flesh come up on the insides of my arms. I couldn't help thinking that just under the skin, even on me, pale as I am, veins ran with red blood . . . but then a kid called Nigel Kratzman, who lived next to me at the time, started talking about trucks—his favorite subject—and since that didn't interest me, and I was just getting over a cold, I thought I'd better slip away and get some sleep.

None of the others saw me move; I was in the dark, well outside the bright ring of firelight.

That afternoon when the rain came, all the sleeping gear had been shifted into a cliff cave behind the fire. It was high in there, going right up into the cliff itself, but the entrance was almost sealed by sand and I had to drop on my hands and knees to crawl in.

The sleeping bags were arranged in a semicircle like the spokes of a wagon wheel, with the entrance at the center. It was very dark, and I used a flashlight to get settled, but when I switched it off I made sure I could still see outside from where I was lying, to watch the others around the fire.

The flames cast shadows up under their jaws. Their eyes seemed deep and hollow. They looked like a circle of the dead.

The cave disappeared into even deeper darkness behind me, and I was feeling strange about that, so I got out of my sleeping bag and shifted it over against a side wall—but I could still see the light of the fire. I slipped my backpack between the bag and a rock to make a pillow, and felt better because then I was half sitting up. I was like that when the others came in. They fooled around for a while then started to quiet down. The fire burned low and the coals glowed strongly sometimes, then died right away at others. That was the wind, rising and falling. I remember lying there with my eyes so wide open, staring out, that they went dry and I made myself blink to wet them.

I couldn't help feeling there was something wrong about that place.

At some point I must have dozed off because my backpack slipped down and what started everything was when my head fell back against the rock. But no rock ever sounded like that—a dull gonging sound, deep, not loud, like the echo in an empty fuel drum when it's been kicked.

I did not move a muscle. I lay there thinking someone was behind me in that darkness. But nothing happened. No movement. No voice. I started to count in my head. Ten. Twenty. Thirty. Forty. Still nothing, even after I passed a hundred. Then I lifted up my hands, back up together without moving my head or the rest of my body, and my fingers touched stuff like hair—fine and wiry—and beyond that, something cold and hard.

I pulled my hands back and reached for my flashlight, then I rolled on my stomach so I could see. Almost right in front of my face was a web of hairy roots that hung down from the blackness, from the cave ceiling I guess. When I pushed the roots away I could see what looked like the sides of a smooth black rock or boulder, but when I touched it and tapped it this thing was a big pot, sitting on a ledge of rock in the cave wall—a big metal pot.

It reminded me of the pots illustrated in comics sometimes with a white hunter sitting inside and cannibals standing around with bones in their noses waiting for him to boil. I told this to the TV crews who climbed down the cliffs to the beach the next day. I told them about the pot and the cannibal comics and that name seemed to stick. When the papers came out they called it the "cannibal pot."

I got up on my knees and crawled out of my sleeping bag but I didn't say anything. I shined my light around the top of the pot and there was a lid with a handle on it. Dirt and small rocks were all over this. The lid had a lot of weight as if there was suction from inside. I yanked hard, pulling back with my body, and the lid came away, sliding toward me an inch or two. Kneeling up on the ledge, I got above the thing and shined my light down into the gap but the stink coming out was terrible. A hot, musty smell.

I pulled my head back and must have made some sound because then I heard the others talking and saw flashlight beams flicking around the roof of the cave. Someone had spotted me on the ledge.

I didn't care that they were watching me. I really wanted to see what was inside that pot and pushed the lid back a bit more so I could look in without getting too close. I could see a rectangular shape, or a corner of a rectangular shape—and another thing. I couldn't make out what it was.

A few kids were behind me by this time, saying "What's going on?" so I put my hand inside and groped around. The thing I touched was stiff with a rough sort of surface that felt like dry leather. I remember thinking this could be anything and I would have to wash my hands later, then I picked it up between two fingers and lifted it out. Everyone saw what it was as it came over the edge of the pot, and right away I threw it down onto my sleeping bag. It was a human hand.

There was a hell of an uproar. Flashlights were shining everywhere. Then Kratzman got a stick (it might have been the handle of a specimen net) and started poking at the hand. It was lying there, right in the middle of my sleeping bag. While this was going on, in came the teachers, Ericson and Schuler. They must have heard the noise.

Ericson pushed some kids out of the way and said "Settle down here." He was so cool in front of his girlfriend.

Kratzman said, "Look!" and put the stick under the hand, flicking it up. Ericson grabbed at it with a kind of reflex action. He juggled it in midair for a second then saw what it was. Next thing he fainted.

Schuler got a flashlight and had a good look, first at the hand, then inside the pot. She said to leave everything alone, not to touch the pot because it could need to be fingerprinted. She was already thinking this was a crime scene and worried about looking after the evidence. She put the hand in a plastic specimen bag we had brought to collect marine samples.

By this time it was early the next day, which was Sunday. We were due to be picked up by bus at 3 P.M. Schuler told us to move away from the ledge where the pot was. She said to try to forget what had happened and get some sleep. She even told some kids it was probably a practical joke. Nobody believed her. Then she went outside and sat by the fire with Ericson. I think he was too ashamed to face us.

As soon as Schuler had gone, what happened was incredible because everyone started flashing their lights over the cave roof making weird shadows and some kids were coughing and choking like they were being strangled. Of course, Kratzman was the one who tried to keep order and issue directions—he was like that, he always had to be in charge. I perched up on the ledge, out of the way, watching, but Kratz really started to get to me after a while.

Anyway, Ericson proved to be good for something. As soon as the sun came up, everyone bundled outside to see Schuler asleep by the fire alone. Ericson had brought his trail bike with him, strapped to the back of the bus. He had only done that to look tough, but it turned out to be useful, because he came back with the police. They poked around a bit, then the TV crews came, and from there the interviews started—lots of them.

Item 3

Radio 6 KR Hamelin 10:05 A.M.
Tuesday, April 15, 1986

Transcript of Press
Conference Tape:
SENIOR SERGEANT RON NORMAN

(Beginning of tape)

UNIDENTIFIED MALE VOICE: . . . more about the hand?

SGT. NORMAN: Yes. We know a little more. There is still considerable guesswork. We believe it's the hand of a female, white. Aged somewhere between fourteen and eighteen.

MALE VOICE: Can you establish a cause of death?

SGT. NORMAN: Well . . . no . . . but a bone of the fourth finger was broken, and had not knitted at the time of death. This could mean there was violence or it may have no connection with the death at all. It's a left hand, by the way.

MALE VOICE: Drew Morefield. The *Observer.* Sorry, Sergeant, I don't quite follow you. Hadn't the hand been severed from the body?

SGT. NORMAN: Yes.

Observer: Well then surely . . . there can't be any doubt about death by violence?

SGT. NORMAN: Not necessarily.

Observer: What are you suggesting? That a girl was walking along and her hand simply dropped off . . . and then fell in a big iron pot?

(Laughter)

SGT. NORMAN: I'm not suggesting anything of the sort. The hand had been removed at the wrist by a series of very small cuts. Possibly these were made with a serrated knife. More likely the sharp edge of a shell or even a stone. The cuts are jagged. They were probably made some months after death. Certainly the removal of the hand was not the cause of death, if that's what you're getting at.

FEMALE VOICE: Audrey Willis. *The Weekend Courier.* Sergeant, it's what *you're* getting at that's unclear. *(laughter)* What I have so far is that a girl has died, possibly violently, and that some months after her death somebody came along and cut the left hand off with a piece of razor-sharp shell. True?

SGT. NORMAN: Yes. That's right. But of course the corpse had been mummified. First.

Courier: Mummified? Like in Egypt?

SGT. NORMAN: Similar, I suppose . . .

MALE VOICE: Sergeant . . . if you're . . . sorry . . . Luke Collins, *Strand Magazine* . . . if you're serious, this could be some sort of cult killing. Are you serious?

SGT. NORMAN: Yes. I'm serious. But I wonder how many of you are, judging by the questions you're asking. How about a little more order, more logic?

Observer: What questions do you suggest Sergeant?

SGT. NORMAN: What? Am I supposed to ask the questions and answer them too?

(Laughter)

Okay. Okay. Try this:
Question: How long has the victim been deceased?
Answer: Over two hundred and fifty, maybe three hundred years.

(Silence)

Courier: Three hundred years? But you said this was a white girl. Three hundred years predates white settlement by—

SGT. NORMAN: Exactly. Maybe this white girl lived here and

met her death over a hundred and fifty years before the traditional dates of European settlement. At least well before 1788 and the so-called First Fleet.

Strand: Are you satisfied with the dating of the evidence? Could there be an error?

SGT. NORMAN: Of course there could be. We can only be accurate to say, give or take fifty years. The dating was done by our forensic people brought up from Perth. An independent team from the university is on it now. They are checking skin and blood samples. There's plenty of skin. Blood's only like trace elements. Nothing much there . . .

MALE VOICE: If those dates are correct, how do you account for the victim . . . this girl . . . being here?

SGT. NORMAN: Good. We're starting to come up with some decent questions, aren't we? Well, the answer is probably a shipwreck. No transcontinental flights in those days.

(Laughter)

But history is out of my area. Some of the maritime archaeologists working on this say she could have been Dutch. Lot of Dutch shipping up this coast in the 1600s.

Strand: Do they think that she could have been killed by natives?

SGT. NORMAN: Can't say. The evidence suggests she lived off the land for some time after her arrival. Fingernails were very worn and broken, indicating a fair bit of manual labor. Probably digging or foraging for food. Maybe she lived with the local natives as a tribal member. But it's very unlikely that they would have killed her. I believe natives only mummified people who were highly respected. They wouldn't want to murder her, then keep the body.

Strand: Do you know how they actually preserved their mummies?

SGT. NORMAN: No. But some of our local Aborigines might.

Strand: Well, do you know why the hand was cut off? Why it was in that pot? You couldn't call the pot an Aboriginal artefact. It's made of iron.

SGT. NORMAN: Too many things to answer there. I'll try one at a time. First, an Aboriginal friend told me the hand could have been worn as a good-luck charm. Quite common to wear a part of a loved one around the neck or carry bones or a finger in a "charm bag." This was supposed to keep away evil spirits.

Strand: But the pot . . . ? Why the "cannibal" pot? Any more about that?

SGT. NORMAN: Yes. We have a little more. We certainly chop and change, don't we? I want to say from the outset this cannibal thing is false. At least probably false. There's no evidence of cannibalism. I mean that name has got around now. It began as a kid's joke . . .

(Pause)

The pot itself is pretty basic. Black iron. About two feet in diameter with a lid that fits quite snugly. There is a strong handle attached at the shoulders where it bulges out.

Courier: Does it have a manufacturer's name anywhere? A place of origin? Date?

SGT. NORMAN: No. Nothing like that.

MALE VOICE: First reports said there was wood underneath. Had it been on a fire?

SGT. NORMAN: Can't say as yet. Scrapings have been taken from the exterior. But the wood found under it—what was left of it—certainly hadn't been for burning. It seemed to be some sort of support or base . . . similar to the wooden pallet used to move heavy loads—that sort of thing.

Courier: Any distinguishing marks? Paint?

SGT. NORMAN: No. It certainly didn't say THIS SIDE UP like a packing case. Our forensic team believes the wood is oak. European. And when that finally rots you're talking in centuries.

Observer: Can you make any connection between the pot and the hand?

SGT. NORMAN: None at all.

Observer: What about the man's wallet they found? Wasn't that in the pot too?

SGT. NORMAN: There was no wallet found—

Courier: But that was reported from the outset—

SGT. NORMAN: Yes, and incorrectly. It was not a wallet. A leather-bound book was found. Handwritten. I suppose it was called a wallet because the leather folds around the pages. Similar to a legal folio. We don't have much on that yet. It was given to our handwriting people but

they couldn't make heads or tails of it and it's been flown
to Perth. Too soon for any outcome. You'll have to wait.
But we're hoping it answers quite a few questions—

Strand: Sergeant, could this be a hoax? I mean the Messenger
kid, could he have planted all this there as some sort of
joke? You know kids . . .

SGT. NORMAN: Sure. I thought that . . . everyone thought
that. But nobody could fake that wood. It's been sitting
there, in exactly the same place, for centuries. And the
hand, it's as real as mine. But there is one thing about
the evidence. We believe it's been tampered with . . .
something removed. I can't say what exactly, not at this
time, sorry.

MALE VOICE: You can't just leave us like that. More?

SGT. NORMAN: Well . . . maybe the kids know more . . .

MALE VOICE: Do you think . . .

(End of tape)

Item 4

Messenger, Midway Roadhouse

I went back to school the day after Sergeant Norman did the
interview on the radio, but the first period had hardly started
when the principal came to the class asking for the students
who went on the biology trip to report immediately to the
staff room.

Only about fifteen of those kids were at school that day.
Another five or six were still away. I couldn't understand why

anyone except me needed time off—I was the one who actually found the hand and picked it up—but these kids who had nothing to do with it stayed home. For instance Nigel Kratzman, who lived next door to me, took two days off, the same as I did, but I saw what he was doing. He wasn't taking a rest to recover from shock—he was up to his elbows in grease, stripping an engine. And the others were just as bad. When they were going to the staff room, they talked and laughed about how "sick" they had been and made a joke of the whole thing, so I dropped back and let them go on.

That school, Hamelin High, is only a miserable country school with a few wooden buildings, each one with a rickety veranda down the side. From the veranda you could see the dirt playground and the scraggly trees around it. About sixty or seventy kids went there and most of them came in from ranches and farms in the area.

Hardly any kids lived in Hamelin itself, which was not much more than a dozen buildings on either side of the main highway. Only one building was brick and concrete and that was the Shire Council Chambers with the courtroom and library. I was never in the courtroom (although Nigel Kratzman was—I will include more about that later) but the library was all right. I used to go there after school sometimes. I didn't do that so often because if I did I would have to hitch home, since there was only one bus going down my way after 3 o'clock. The Council Chambers was a solid sort of building, and the library there was cool and quiet inside. The library at the school wasn't much good—the books were childish.

The staff room was at the end of one of the verandas. It was a big room with windows looking out over the scrub. When I went in I saw the other kids sitting around the teachers' lunch table in the middle of the room. The two teachers from the camp were there, Ericson and Schuler, but not together, and the principal was in the corner near the coffee urn. She was talking to Sergeant Norman. I slipped in while no one noticed but didn't take a chair up at the table. I sat behind.

After a minute the principal said, "Well, I'm sure you all know Sergeant Norman. I'll leave you with him. Mr. Ericson and Ms. Schuler, you stay too, if you don't mind. I'll look after your classes." Then she left and the sergeant moved away from the urn and stood near the table. He asked if everyone was feeling better and had settled down since the camp. Kids nodded and looked at each other or at their hands so they didn't have to catch his eye. He said congratulations were in order for how sensible they had been "under the circumstances" and that showed "how mature teenagers could be," etc.

I started to get the idea he was buttering them up for something. Then he said, "I'm afraid we aren't out of the woods yet—or out of the cave." It was meant as a joke, but everyone looked blank, waiting for the punch line. "I need your help," he said. "We seem to have some missing evidence. I thought one of you could supply that . . ."

Nobody had a clue what he was talking about, but they were all trying to look intelligent. "I asked somebody along to meet you," he said, turning to the corner. "Mr. Charles Sunrise from the mission. I want him to explain a few things. Maybe then you'll understand why you're here."

I leaned out from behind the kids in front of me and looked over to the corner. There was someone I had missed before, maybe because the principal had been in the way. From behind the urn an old Aborigine stood up and he came forward near the table.

There were plenty of Aborigines at this school, and

some Asians too. The Asians were descended from divers who used to collect sea slugs off the coast; some were Malays, some Chinese, but they all looked alike. I couldn't tell the difference and didn't have anything to do with them. Of course, the Aborigines were in this country all the time, so I can't say they're exactly foreign, just different. The Abo kids from near the town were okay and clean enough, but the ones who came in from the countryside weren't the same. They needed a wash and looked as if they'd cut your throat. If one came near me I'd move. They didn't care. After school (that is, if they turned up at all) they'd disappear back into the bush where they came from. In my opinion it was better that way.

This one Sergeant Norman introduced looked like he was from out of town. At least, I didn't think I had seen him before. He was maybe sixty or seventy. He had thick gray hair, like a steel scouring pad but he kept his head low so I couldn't see his face. His shirt had red and white checks with the sleeves torn out and open down the front. I saw his bony ribs. He had long gray pants but no belt. I slipped down in my chair a bit and could see under the table. He had bare feet covered in lumps and calluses; the toes were long and twisted in different directions. He looked the type who came in from the bush or from the mission, like the sergeant said. I'd heard how they hung about drinking cheap wine near the dump on the edge of town and I thought, what the hell would he want here at the school?

Then the sergeant was talking. He said "Charlie, are you ready?" and the old Abo nodded. He was holding a cup of something hot and I could see his fingers, bent around the cup like claws. His hands were deformed, but the skin was black and shiny as polished leather.

"Tell them what I asked you in for, Charlie," the Sergeant said. "Come on. I'll hold your tea if you like."

He took the cup, then this Charlie lifted his head. I felt my stomach turn over. His mouth was open, ready to speak, and with his missing teeth in the front and his wide nostrils, his face was horrible. I saw his eyes were black and half closed and around them watery pink veins.

I looked away to the window until he started to speak. He said, "The sergeant asked me to talk about the hand in the cave. It came from my people, but is not one of them. It is a white hand. All my life I never saw such a thing. I told the sergeant this hand must be very important . . . the person from far away . . . another place . . ."

He stopped and I saw him look at the sergeant, who was shaking his head. "A bit too fast, Charlie," he said. "Slow down. Tell them what the hand is first, then maybe where it came from."

I heard a chair scrape back, and the next thing I saw was Kratzman standing right next to Charlie and giving him his seat at the table. The sergeant nodded and grinned, so Charlie sat down with the others, and Kratz went off to one side, near the urn, and stood where the principal had been.

Charlie started again. He had a strange high voice that made you listen to every word. "My people, they don't do so many of the old things anymore. Those days are all gone. When the sergeant shows me that hand I says that to him. I says I could not do that anymore. No one of my people could. Long ago, maybe over a hundred years ago, yes. The fella whose hand that was, he must be dead over a hundred years. More. In those days they take the fella who died and put his body high in a tree. My people make a place up there in the branches. A flat place. High up in the sun. They put leaves over the body. Sweet and fresh. Not too many to stop the sun working. Some might put marks on the tree as signs. Cut them in the bark to show this was a special place. A spirit place. Then my people go. They might leave one or two to watch and come back to take the dry body later. Or take the bones. These bones could tell about trouble. Or an enemy coming. Sometimes my people would keep a part of this body, like the jaw maybe. Or a part of a hand. A finger. These were sacred things for important people who died . . ."

When he stopped, the room was very quiet. No one was fidgeting. All eyes were on him. I thought he had forgotten what he was going to say next.

Sergeant Norman said "Go on, Charlie," and he started talking again, but he was turned to one side, more to the outside. His voice was not so high anymore. It seemed harder to say the words.

". . . Maybe this hand was from another place. A spirit place. Maybe an ancestor who went away and came back. Or a dead child. They come back. Maybe this might be the hand of a spirit child come back. But I have never seen such a thing. Not in my life. Not a white hand. Never. I will not talk anymore about these things."

I thought he had finished for sure, but Sergeant Norman leaned over and whispered in his ear. He listened, his head well down, then he started to nod slowly. He seemed to agree with something that was said.

His voice came again, but very muffled. "The sergeant asked me about the hand. I told him what I told you here. He showed me the hand. I never seen this before. But I know"—he lifted his head when he said this—"something is not there. Off one finger there is something gone . . . The sergeant asked me about marks on one finger. That is wax. Hard wax . . . very old . . . wax that held something there, on the finger. I have spoken enough. I will not speak anymore, not about the sacred things of my people."

He stopped speaking and put his head on his hands.

The sergeant whispered something again and Charlie looked up with a grin. In a minute he had a steaming cup in his twisted hand and the sergeant stood behind him, with one arm around his shoulder.

"Charlie said quite a lot. He's not too comfortable in places like this. And he doesn't like talking about tribal matters much either. Especially death. So I won't go on and upset him anymore. But I called you here to listen to him for one reason. I believe he is right. There is something missing from the hand. Something important. Does anyone know what I'm talking about?"

Nobody said anything.

"No? Well . . . the black substance Charlie identified on the finger of the hand was wax. Wax from the native bee. This wax had been molded around the fourth finger on that hand—the wedding ring finger—like your mothers'. You know what I mean?"

Some kids nodded.

"I think there was a ring on that hand, and I think it was there when you found it. Probably it had native wax stuck around it to protect it, or maybe to hide it. But when the hand was tossed about by you kids in the cave, that wax cracked and broke off. And then the ring fell off too. Or was pulled off. You know what I mean?"

There was silence.

"I asked Charlie Sunrise here to try and tell you how important these findings are. If there is a ring missing from—"

But Charlie's voice cut in, "We don't care about rings. My people don't want that ring."

"I know, Charlie," the sergeant said. "I'm just trying to tell these kids that if there is a ring, finding it might help us clear up who the owner was. We might be able to use it in working out how she came to be with your people. Maybe when too. Now is there anything to tell me about this business?"

Nobody seemed to know. One kid said that we weren't all at school. Maybe a kid who was away knew something. Another kid said how the hand had been tossed around at first, then handled again by Ericson and Schuler before it was put in the specimen bag. That was true. Kratzman came forward and said, "Maybe it fell off and is still in the sand on the floor of the cave." But the sergeant shook his head.

"No . . . we sifted the floor sand for hours. Nothing. Listen. I'm not accusing you kids of anything. I want you to know that, but this is really important. You understand this is probably one of the most valuable pieces of evidence in this investigation."

Then I said, "Is this ring gold—or what? Is it worth money?"

I saw the sergeant was a bit surprised. "Well, it might be," he said. "But that's not the point. That's not why we want to find it. It's value is as an archaeological relic—a piece of a historical jigsaw puzzle."

Then he said, "You're Messenger, aren't you? The one who found the hand. Interesting."

I don't know why he said my name, and the word "interesting," but when he did everyone turned to stare at me. I saw that Charlie staring too, as if he could see straight through me, through my skin and to my bones beneath.

I felt my face go hot as fire, and right at that moment Sunrise dropped his cup and boiling tea went everywhere.

Later, on the way home, the bus kids said it was my fault the meeting ended and they had to go back to class. They said that one look at me would make anyone sick. Kratzman said nothing. He never took my side, even though we were neighbors. He just sat in the back seat, grinning. I hated the lot of them.

From the Western Mirror, *April 22, 1986*

Cannibal Pot Document Puzzle: No Link to Human Hand

Perth, Tuesday. Maritime archaeologists believe that a leather-bound journal, found by a schoolboy, could be over three hundred years old.

The journal was flown to Perth's Institute of Maritime Archaeology shortly after its discovery in a Murchison River cave last week.

Initially reported to be a man's leather wallet, the item is now believed to be the journal of Dutch sailors shipwrecked off the Western Australian coast as early as 1650.

Hope Michaels, Director of the Institute of Maritime Archaeology, has given investigation into the journal's authenticity and origin top research priority. Speaking from the Institute yesterday, Dr. Michaels said, "If this proves to be genuine, we have a major archaeological find on our hands. The person who wrote this was the equivalent of a seventeenth-century man on the moon. This is like a three-hundred-year-old time capsule he left behind. Of course, it could prove to be more of a Pandora's box, depending on what we learn when we translate the text. If present indications prove correct, what we find may not be too pretty."

At this stage of the investigation she could not establish

any meaningful links between the journal, the human hand, and the iron "cannibal pot" in which the items were found by schoolboy Steven Messenger. Responding to suggestions that certain evidence had yet to be surrendered to the research team, Dr. Michaels believed there was a missing item, probably a ring, but "archaeologists were generally patient people" and she would adopt a wait-and-see attitude.

In the meantime she hoped the public would consider contributing toward the erection of a monument or plaque commemorating Messenger's historic find.

According to Dr. Michaels, an interim report on the Institute's investigation into the journal should be available in late May.

Item 6

Messenger, Midway Roadhouse

My mother brings home newspapers and magazines that people leave in the Midway Roadhouse restaurant where she works. Everyone who goes there calls her Rene. Her real name is Irene.

The truckers yell, "Hey, Rene, coffee over here!" or "What's keeping ya' so long, Rene?"

She brought home the *Western Mirror* that ran the article saying there should be a monument to me. I read it to her while she was making supper.

She laughed and said, "Where would they put a monument around here?"

Good question.

The three of us, my mother and father and myself, live right next door to the Roadhouse truck stop on Highway

One, about thirty miles south of Hamelin, which is like saying thirty miles south of nowhere. When people see the Roadhouse sign they say, "The Midway—midway to where?"

That's another good question.

It would be easy to describe this place, but easier still to draw. On a piece of paper make two parallel lines about a quarter-inch apart going straight up the middle, from bottom to top. That's Highway One. An asphalt strip. Dead straight.

Over to the left print OCEAN CLIFF, and to the right DESERT. Don't show any trees or rocks. No creeks or gullies. Nothing like that. Only sand. Sometimes this comes from the west, from the cliff tops, sometimes from the east, off the desert. It depends on the wind, and that blows all the time.

Highway One never seems to be stable. If it's not drifting with sand, it's shimmering with heat—putting up little wispy hazes that blur in the distance to make lakes, or thick forests or silvery mountains, or even skyscrapers. They're all lies, of course. Only illusions.

But to finish that drawing, add a rectangle about halfway up Highway One on the left. Make it about a half-inch by an inch, with the long side on the highway. That's the Midway Roadhouse.

It's the usual—garage, diner, a couple of motel rooms. And the sign. Twenty-four hours a day, year in year out, that sign blinks away the same message: VACANCY . . . VACANCY . . . VACANCY . . .

Around the Roadhouse are half a dozen mobile homes, the ones they move with a semitrailer tractor. A barbed-wire fence encloses each one, but it's only a single strand. Nobody is fooled—it doesn't keep anything in or out.

At night, in the dead quiet, the trailer units seem to creep in closer to the Roadhouse lights looking for protection.

Only two of those units have ever been occupied. The

Kratzmans (Nigel and his mother) live in one, and ours is the other.

Our trailer would be simple to draw too—but there'd be no point. It's exactly what anyone would expect. An aluminum rectangle with a flat roof. Facing the road is the living room and kitchen, in the middle is a bathroom, and behind that are two bedrooms. The whole thing sits on twelve steel pipes, two feet above the sand. It's bolted down with forty-eight bolts. I've counted every one.

I often sit outside the screen door on the front steps, looking across the highway at the desert. Or I go out the back and sit on the steps there. I can't see the edge of the cliffs because of the low scrub, but way over is the ocean. It's not blue, or even green—it's gray, blasted by the wind into white caps that smash at the cliffs below us.

I sometimes wonder if the sea is eating away there, bit by bit, and maybe one night the units will tilt and slowly sink into the sand, and the Roadhouse and even Highway One will simply vanish forever, undermined, or swallowed up by the sea beneath. If that happened, at least I would never have to look at the VACANCY sign again.

Anyway, then a new cliff would appear, with a fine, fresh, sharp edge—clean.

So this is not the sort of place they would pick to build a monument. If the sand didn't get it, the ocean would. Sane people only stop here for gasoline or one of Rene's burgers.

We live on the highway because of my father. He's a trucker—always driving north. I don't know what the attraction of "north" is, nor does my mother, but ever since I can remember my family has been moving farther and farther up Highway One. I wonder what will be there when we reach the top? Disneyland?

The only reason we stayed here at the Midway so long—

about two years—is that my mother said I needed some high school education if I was ever going to get a job. But I know when we're about to move again. My father takes on contracts that are farther and farther away. He stays away longer too.

Things were shaping up like that when I found the ring. My father had been gone for weeks, much longer than usual. I guessed that when he came back the pressure would be on to pack up and leave. But then the ring turned up and I said to myself, "No matter what happens, I'm going to have this. I'm going to keep it until I'm ready to give it up."

That particular night (the night I found the ring), I was lying on my bed, staring out at the motel sign, when my mother came to my door. She wanted to know if I was all right. I had been sick with a bad cold and there had been so much hype about being upset by finding the hand that I think she was worried.

"I'm all right," I said. "Just lying here."

She asked me if I wanted a drink. I said no and she turned to go, but as she did, her foot caught in my sleeping bag, left on the floor since the camp.

She said, "You better clean that up before there's an accident," and the door clicked shut.

I am a very tidy person. Very orderly. I don't like any kind of mess. That bag had been left out deliberately so I could roll it up tight. I never had the chance to do that on the trip. With all the goings on, it was just stuffed into its drawstring cover. I was annoyed I had forgotten to fix it, and now it was busting out all over my bedroom floor. I got up, spread it out straight, then rolled it neatly. I reached over and picked up the empty cover, giving it a shake to get rid of any loose sand.

Then something hit the floor. The thing sounded quite

light—it bounced once or twice on the bare boards and disappeared under my bed. I finished pushing the sleeping bag into its cover, pulled the strings tight, and got down to see what had made the noise. It sounded like a coin. Groping around in the darkness, I felt something cold.

It was a black ring, maybe three-quarters of an inch in diameter. When I scratched the surface with my thumb, black stuff got under my nail. I remember getting up off the floor, holding it up higher to the light, and scratching at it some more. When I saw gold underneath, my stomach gave a heave. I knew what I had found—the ring off the mummified hand. The black was the wax Sergeant Norman and that Charlie Sunrise had told everyone about.

I sat down on the bed, looking at the ring lying in my palm. I could see part of the golden band quite clearly. The rest was still covered in the lumpy black wax. Maybe, like the sergeant said, the dead girl had covered the ring to hide or even protect it. When she died and her hand shrank the ring came off. Well, it didn't really. It stayed on for as long as she had been dead, maybe hundreds of years, until Kratzman started to toss the hand around like a Frisbee. Then the ring fell off. Right into my sleeping bag. I couldn't believe it.

I was thinking of showing it to my mother, but I stopped, right there in my bedroom doorway. That's when I said those things to myself. I wouldn't give the ring away. I'd keep it for a while.

I got some clean clothes and went to the bathroom. I locked the door and found an old toothbrush in the cupboard under the basin, then I put the ring on the edge of the shower, undressed, and got in. With the shower running, first I scrubbed under my fingernails, then the ring, until all the black wax was gone. Little by little I could see what it was really like.

The band was deep yellow gold with a dark red stone set in it. The stone wasn't raised at all. Not like today's rings with the stone set in a claw. And the stone wasn't cut into facets either. It was polished smooth, more like a shiny bead. It was the simplest, most beautiful thing I had ever seen. I thought, "I'll keep this until I'm ready." But then I had to get out of the shower because my mother was yelling "Don't waste the water." There is a water truck that comes down from town to fill the tanks.

Back in my room I shut the door and turned on the reading lamp over my bed. The stone in the ring caught the light, but it didn't sparkle, it glowed, deep inside. I wondered whether it was a ruby, or maybe a garnet—I knew they were red.

The stone in the ring was the color of blood.

Received Wednesday, May 28, 1986

Interim Report on a Leather-bound Manuscript Located in Cliff Cave 327, Murchison River District, April 13, 1986

PREPARED BY DR. HOPE MICHAELS,
DIRECTOR, WESTERN AUSTRALIAN INSTITUTE
OF MARITIME ARCHAEOLOGY

Introduction
In response to various requests for an investigation into objects found in Cliff Cave 327, Murchison River District, commonly called the "Cannibal Pot" Cave, the following is a preliminary report on one object: a leather-bound, handwritten

manuscript. From the outset, the reader's attention should be drawn to the following:

A. Given the limited time available for research, this report is in no way an exhaustive or final analysis of the manuscript or its contents.

B. Because of the manuscript's delicate state, only the first few pages have been analyzed. It is considered imperative that the manuscript be photographed under controlled conditions before further handling for purposes of translation takes place.

C. This institute specializes in maritime archaeology. Any aspect of the manuscript which does not pertain to this field of research is therefore beyond our professional competence and has been duly noted in the report.

1.00. Analysis of the Item

The item under analysis is a form of book, comprising 120 pages, stitched in a fabric cover, the whole encased in a tooled leather jacket, which has been called a wallet.

The jacket measures 14.5 by 10.14 inches, average thickness 1 inch and opens by means of leather flaps that fold back, similar to an envelope or document wallet. This Institute is not able to identify the leather type. Condition of the leather is dry and brittle. One of the research team referred to it as "fragile as a wafer."

A major distinguishing feature of the leather jacket is an insignia:

V.O.C.

which is tooled into its center. The letters (3.5 inches high by 4.25 inches across) are of the utmost significance in identifying the item. The logo V.O.C. was the insignia of the United East India Company *(de Vereenigde Oost Indishe Compag-*

nie), a Dutch trading enterprise operating mainly between the Netherlands and Java in the seventeenth and eighteenth centuries. Many of its vessels came in contact with the west coast of Australia during this time.

1.01. The interior fabric covering the manuscript is sailcloth (unbleached canvas) with a thread count of thirty by twenty-five threads per square inch. This fabric is badly soiled and fragile, suggesting great age and considerable handling. The size of this internal cover is 13.7 by 9.3 inches, allowing it to fit into the external leather jacket or wallet. The fabric cover has been stitched through to bind the internal pages. This binding, which has almost completely decomposed, is of twine.

Samples of the cover fabric and twine have been dispatched for detailed analysis to the Peabody Museum, Salem, Massachusetts, which specializes in sailcloth dating.

In the meanwhile, however, sufficient evidence exists to state with some reliability that this is a ship's logbook from the seventeenth or eighteenth century.

1.02. The manuscript itself is of heavy gauge paper, probably handmade. Pages are approximately 13 by 9 inches, with rough edges. They are badly discolored and exceptionally brittle. All pages have sprung from the stitched binding.

Although only three pages were examined, in the center of each appeared the watermark V.O.C. and beneath that the number 1627, which is believed to be the date of manufacture.

2.00. Analysis of the Text
The document is handwritten in Gothic script. Sheets are written on both sides. It is interesting to note that on the right-hand, or facing pages, the handwriting is relatively even and ordered, while that on the left-hand side, or back, of each

page is poorly formed and disorderly by comparison, suggesting a more hurried and nervous style.

Continuity in ideas is only gained by reading each right-hand page, and then each left-hand page, in order. The research team believes that all right-hand pages were written first. Several of the left-hand pages at the end of the manuscript have no writing on them.

Two writing mediums have been used: initially a black ink and later a paler, purple ink.

2.01. The language used is Old Dutch. This proved a translation problem for the research team. While several members have some grasp of that language through contact with relics from Dutch wrecks, none was capable of a free and accurate translation. Furthermore, the fragile condition of the pages did not lend itself to handling for this purpose. Therefore only a cursory attempt at translation of the first three pages, intended to establish the authorship and purpose of the document, was undertaken.

3.00. Evidence of Authorship

Early in the text the author identifies himself as Wouter Loos, aged 24, a Dutch soldier and survivor of the V.O.C. vessel *Batavia*, which was wrecked off the Western Australian coast on June 4, 1629. The research team considers this claim of authorship to be historically probable.

3.01. The fate of the V.O.C. vessel *Batavia* has been well known to historians and maritime archaeologists for many years—mainly through the preservation of accounts of the wreck, and of its aftermath, provided by the V.O.C. Commandeur aboard the vessel, Francisco Pelsaert.[1]

---

1. This title was an honorary one given to merchants of some standing in seventeenth-century Holland. It does not correspond to the English naval rank commander—Ed.

Pelsaert records that the *Batavia* ran aground on Houtman's Abrolhos Rocks, off the Western Australian coast, in the early hours of June 4, 1629. Most of the passengers and crew, numbering about 260 persons, survived the wreck and landed safely upon barren islands nearby. Pelsaert, in a desperate attempt to find help, managed to reach Java in an open boat, returning after a round trip of fourteen weeks with a vessel to rescue the remaining survivors. However, to his horror, he found that over 120 men, women, and children, having lived through the rigors of shipwreck and near starvation, had subsequently been brutally murdered by members of the *Batavia* crew and other malcontents.

In his journal, the original of which is kept in The Hague, Pelsaert faithfully records every detail of the capture, trial, and execution of the guilty parties, which he conducted. Before returning to Java, Pelsaert personally supervised the hanging of the murderers on the spot, having first had their hands cut off.

Of utmost significance to this report is Pelsaert's journal entry stating that he had shown mercy to two of the guilty. These men were not to die but to be cast away in a small skiff with some provisions and trading goods. One of these castaways was a seventeen-year-old youth, Jan Pelgrom, convicted of rape and murder. The other was a soldier, Wouter Loos, who identifies himself as the author of the manuscript under study.

3.02. Pelsaert's journal states that Loos and Pelgrom were abandoned to their fate, on November 16, 1629. Dating of the sailcloth cover and the V.O.C. watermark on the manuscript (1627) is consistent with events dated and recorded by Pelsaert.

3.03. The Murchison River is a reasonable location for the discovery of evidence relating to Wouter Loos and Jan Pel-

The hanging of the *Batavia* murderers, as illustrated in an account of the events, *Unlucky Voyage*, written in 1649.

grom. Although considerably farther north than Pelsaert's journal indicates (perhaps the Hutt River region), it is possible that the castaways managed to sail some distance northward in the skiff Pelsaert had provided. Alternatively, they could have landed and trekked up the coast.

3.04. It is interesting to note that authors and scholars have continued to believe that Loos and Pelgrom may have survived the horrors of the unknown continent.

Henrietta Drake-Brockman, the definitive authority on the wreck of the *Batavia*, wrote of Loos and Pelgrom:

Their names are remembered in history, not by reason of their crimes but because they were the first two white men recorded to have lived on the continent of Australia.[2]

Hugh Edwards, a journalist and diver who participated in locating the *Batavia* wreck in 1963, considered that the fate of the castaways would never be known:

> Their story may be among the most interesting sagas of early Australian history; but we will not know it, for they were never seen or heard of again. . . . They were swallowed up by the huge, mysterious, unknown continent called the Southland . . . so far from the windmills and green fields of Holland . . .[3]

Some authorities including the self-styled anthropologist, Daisy Bates, believe that they recognized European features in Aborigines of the Western Australian coastal tribes. Bates records:

> I also found traces of types distinctly Dutch. When Pelsaert marooned two white criminals on the mainland of Australia in 1627 [*sic*] these Dutchmen had probably been allowed to live with the natives, and it may be that they and their progeny journeyed far along the river highways for I found these types as far out as the headwaters of the Gascoyne and the Murchison. There was no mistaking the flat heavy Dutch face, curly fair hair, and heavy, stocky build.[4]

2. *Voyage to Disaster*, Angus & Robertson, London, 1963, p. 49.
3. *Island of Angry Ghosts*, Angus & Robertson, London, 1979; pp. 78–79.
4. *The Passing of the Aborigines*, Panther, London, 1966, p. 126.

4.00. Content of the Manuscript

At this time it is not appropriate for the research team to provide even a partial translation of the manuscript. There are several reasons for this decision:

a. the research team's limited ability to translate accurately;
b. the inadvisability of handling the manuscript for translation purposes in its present condition;
c. the legal issues involved in ownership of the manuscript (these will be considered in Section 5.00 of this report).

However, in the public interest, the research team wishes to state that:

a. All team members believe the manuscript to be authentic. If this is a hoax, then the persons responsible have access to information and equipment of extreme sophistication.
b. All team members believe the manuscript to be written by Wouter Loos, survivor of the *Batavia* wreck, cast away for murder off the Western Australian coast in 1629.
c. The manuscript appears to be a journal, kept by Loos, detailing his experiences on contact with the mainland.

4.01. Members of the research team have been constantly asked about the connection between the manuscript and other objects found with it in Cliff Cave 327. At this time, team members wish to categorically state that they can make no accurate assessment of why, or how, the objects came to be in that place. Independent research teams, including maritime archaeologists, anthropologists, and forensic scientists, will continue to examine the individual objects discovered and report on findings as such information is processed.

The research team does feel, however, that the most often-asked questions relating to the discovery of a mummified human hand should be considered here:

a. No mention of a human hand could be found in the early pages of the manuscript.

b. No evidence exists that the hand in question could be one that was deliberately amputated at the time of the *Batavia* murderers' execution.

c. No evidence exists of a woman being cast away with Loos and Pelgrom. If the hand in question was taken from a woman, her origin is unknown.

d. No links have been made between the discovery of the human hand and reports of missing persons in the Lower Murchison district.

5.00. Claimants to the Manuscript

Although this Institute will make various recommendations to the Heritage Minister under the Historic Shipwrecks Act (1976), the following could be claimants of the objects discovered in Cliff Cave 327:

a. Steven Messenger, the student who found the iron pot and other items; his parents, guardians, or those acting under his power of attorney.

b. The Government of Western Australia.

c. The Commonwealth Government of Australia.

d. The Government of the Netherlands, which still controls all property rights of the V.O.C.

6.00. Conclusions

The research team believes that the document under study is an authentic seventeenth-century manuscript, probably a journal detailing contact with the Australian mainland, handwritten by Wouter Loos, cast away for the crime of murder following the wreck of the *Batavia* in 1629.

The document is considered an invaluable resource and of the utmost significance to various international scientific and historical associations.

7.00. Recommendations
The research team suggests that each of the following be implemented with extreme urgency:

a. that legal claimants of the manuscript be established;
b. that appropriate facilities be made available to photograph the manuscript;
c. that appropriate facilities be made available to treat and preserve the manuscript;
d. that the services of a team of qualified personnel be engaged to translate the manuscript.

Dr. Hope Michaels
Director
Institute of Maritime Archaeology
Perth, Western Australia

Item 8

Messenger, Midway Roadhouse

Exactly how and when the dreams started I can't remember—although the ring featured in every one, I know that. But it was strange because I never actually knew I was dreaming until the night my mother woke me up.

She was sitting on the side of my bed shaking my shoulders. I sat straight up, thinking there was some trouble.

She said, "Are you all right?" I could make out her face by the light of the motel. I mumbled something about my father. I always thought he'd be killed on the road. Then she told me I had been screaming. As soon as she said that, I remembered what had been going on and pulled the sheet up over my chest.

"It's okay," I said, and shook her hands off me. "It was only a bit of a dream."

"Some dream," she said. "I could hear you in my room. You were yelling something about the sky. It's in the sky or up in the sky. It was terrible."

I wanted her to go. "I can't remember," I said. "It was nothing. Go back to bed," and I rolled over to face the wall. I had to do that or else she would see the ring, on a cord around my neck.

I liked that ring from the first time I saw it cleaned up. There was no way anybody else was having it, but I couldn't really wear it either. I would have been asking for trouble turning up at school with a ring on my finger after the visit from Sergeant Norman. So I threaded it on a fine strip of leather and wore it under my shirt. Nobody knew.

I felt my mother get up from the bed. She said, "At least keep yourself covered. I couldn't stand it if you were sick again."

I was always getting colds—I have a weak chest.

I said, "Yes sure," and in a minute she was gone.

I tried to go back to sleep but the ring felt warm against my skin. Outside, the motel sign was blinking . . . VACANCY . . . Then the dream came back . . .

There was the motel sign, flashing against a clear midday sky. And there was Steven Messenger, myself but not myself, in jeans and T-shirt, standing on the burning asphalt, a red wind drifting at his feet. Then came the humming in the wires overhead and this Steven Messenger, this other self, looked up. Something flashed against an unseen sun.

"Spaceship," he said, or "Spacecraft."

The thing spun and dipped as it circled, descending, closer and closer to where he stood. Now, Steven Messenger saw, it was a ring hovering above him, and out of this ring burst a shaft of pure light that shone down to surround him—or envelop him, I should say.

Steven Messenger felt his heels lift from the asphalt and sank, bending in resistance, but the light was too strong and his arms lifted, then his shirt belled out on the air and drifted from him, over his shoulders, and head, up into the whiteness of the light.

He crouched lower, dragging his arms down to find anchorage.

"It is in the sky," he said. "The ring is in the sky," but he could grip nothing. Find no support. Then came a warm slipperiness at his fingers. The same sensation at his feet. He felt the tug of the sea, the ebb of a thick, slow tide.

Steven Messenger looked. He was kneeling in blood. The highway was heavy with it, pushing against his ankles, soaking his jeans. Where he reached down, his fingers were webbed, dripping with blood.

Steven Messenger remembered this, the filth of it, and he remembered also looking up into the white center of the ring, screaming, begging to be taken ... But it was my mother who had brought me back.

Item 9

Photocopied from Famous Australian Murders *by*
Maxwell Futcher (Capricorn Books, Melbourne, 1976)

Chapter 2. Jan Pelgrom: Teenage Murderer of the *Batavia*, pp. 19–22

. . . identifying the characteristics of psychopathic behavior is a complex undertaking. The psychopath does not usually run around the neighborhood waving a banner saying, "Look at me! I've got a problem!" Many are relatively introverted people, at best forming one or two intense, highly possessive relationships.

However, there are more psychopathic types than hairs in Hitler's mustache, and criminal psychologists claim that the socially inadequate psychopath is the one that the pressure of twentieth-century living is producing in ever-increasing numbers.

These socially inadequate psychopaths are often petty criminals whose personal hells of low self esteem have driven them to seek the security and power that membership of a gang can provide. In such cases we must bear in mind that nobody else might consider these people to be inadequate. They need not be rat-faced with underdeveloped biceps and no body hair, for example. What matters is that they think they are inadequate, and furthermore, that's all they think about—unless, of course, they are planning their big chance to prove to the gang, and hence to themselves, that they are the best. Given the right circumstances, this is where socially inadequate psychopaths can become something frightful—psychopathic killers. And this is also where the case of Jan

Pelgrom, seventeen-year-old mass murderer and rapist, may serve as an early example of the type.

There is little doubt that fate dealt Jan Pelgrom an unkind blow. In all likelihood he would have lived the most ordinary of lives, provided the reader considers the life of a cabin boy on a sailing ship in the seventeenth century to be ordinary. Perhaps Pelgrom would have been promoted from this position to become the personal servant of an officer or merchant, eventually dying from plague in some eastern port. We will never know, for on June 4, 1629, Pelgrom's ship, the *Batavia*, ran aground on low-lying islands about forty miles off the Western Australian coast.

It is not necessary to recount all that occurred following the wreck; suffice it to say that over two hundred persons survived and, after a period of early hardship, these people found sufficient food, water, and shelter to exist on the islands while waiting for rescue.

For most, this rescue would not take place—one hundred and twenty of their number were brutally murdered. To understand how this situation could occur, we must further examine the characteristics of a psychopath's behavior.

The ability to sense that his potential victim is in a weak physical or emotional state is an outstanding characteristic of the psychopathic killer. Perhaps there is something of the hyena in him. He needs something, or someone, to bring down his prey first—then he can go in for the finish. The reasoning behind this strategy is obvious: while he considers himself too inadequate to make the initial attack, he is not above claiming the victory for the kill. He needs to prove himself before the pack.

In the case of Jan Pelgrom and the murder of the *Batavia* survivors, two circumstances allowed him to use this "hyena" principle:

1. The shipwreck itself, which demoralized and weakened all persons marooned on the islands. In consideration of what followed, it is reasonable to believe that Pelgrom, the cabin boy, would have been delighted to see so many persons who had once been his superiors now reduced to a common social level.

2. A role model was provided for the young Pelgrom to idolize and impress. Very often in the case of the inadequate psychopath, such a model is evident in the form of an aggressive-charismatic personality type. Simply expressed, a cruel yet powerful charmer. (Although we have previously made light of Hitler, he exemplified this aggressive-charismatic type.)

On the islands, the young Pelgrom fell under the spell of the most senior surviving company officer, Jeronimous Cornelius. It was Cornelius's expressed intention to murder as many survivors as he could, then hijack the hoped-for rescue vessel and take to the high seas, a somewhat romantic idea that was almost accomplished.

Jan Pelgrom volunteered his services as servant to Cornelius, waiting on him hand and foot. There is little doubt that Pelgrom hoped for favors in return—at least to be noticed and enjoy a piece of the action.

Possibly the most telling insight into Pelgrom's character is provided by the murder of a deck boy, named Aldersz, aged about sixteen. Having forced Aldersz to kneel outside his tent, Cornelius informed the ever-present and ever-eager Pelgrom that he could have the pleasure of testing whether a sword blade was keen enough to behead Aldersz with a single blow. Honored and delighted, Pelgrom was about to carry out this act when another villain stepped forward, declaring that Pelgrom was too weak for the task, and did the deed.

The record of this incident at Pelgrom's trial states that

he threw himself on the ground crying with rage because he had been cheated of his kill.

Of course, Pelgrom made up for this in his future raping and stabbing of women and his drowning of children. There is something truly frightful about the character of Jan Pelgrom . . .

Item 10

Photocopied from Select Cases in Australian Crime *by Professor Diana Prior (Brenwood Press, Sydney, 1982)*

. . . We should make a clear distinction between the psychopathic murderer and the person who demonstrates psychopathic behavior at the time of committing murder.

In his somewhat sensationalized work, *Famous Australian Murders,* Max Futcher fails to make that distinction. Futcher argues that the youth, Jan Pelgrom, "might serve as an early example of the psychopathic murderer." Unfortunately, his argument is destroyed when he further states, "fate dealt Jan Pelgrom an unkind blow" and "he would have lived the most ordinary of lives" (p. 20).

The fault with Futcher's argument is that psychopathic murderers are not products of "fate" nor do they live "ordinary" lives. Had Jan Pelgrom been the only killer in this case, Futcher's theory might have been reasonable. But we know that seven men were executed for the *Batavia* murders and two others, Jan Pelgrom and Wouter Loos, were convicted then cast away. Futcher's theory should, therefore, lead us to believe that, by some incredible mischance, not one, but nine psychopathic murderers were aboard the *Batavia* at the time of the wreck, all presumably waiting for their chance to kill.

With all due respect for Max Futcher's scholarship, this would indeed be "fate dealing an unkind blow."

A more reasonable interpretation of the *Batavia* murders could be based upon the theory that the killers exhibited psychopathic behavior patterns at the time of the crimes.

At this point the term *folie à deux* should be introduced. Literally translated, this means "madness together" and it describes a condition in which the insanity of one person seems to affect the mind of another, or even of several other members of a group. In cases of *folie à deux,* if the person who first caused the problem is removed, those who have been affected usually revert to normal behavior patterns.

Perhaps the most famous case of *folie à deux* in modern times is the Jonestown massacre in Guyana. Here, hundreds of members of a religious cult simultaneously committed suicide while under the spell of their fanatical leader. The word *spell* should not suggest that the victims were hypnotized, but that they were temporarily carried away by a form of group hysteria. Certainly, the fact that they had been living together at a remote commune in the South American jungle meant that they were more vulnerable to the forms of power that their cult leader exercised over them. This man managed to raise his unfortunate followers to such a level of fevered anxiety that, before more moderate, stabilizing influences could be brought to bear, all cult members had taken their own lives.*

Elements of this case that could apply to the monstrous circumstances of the *Batavia* mass murders are that, on a re-

---

*Professor Prior is here referring to the Rev. James Warren Jones, who received the Martin Luther King award for services to humanity in January 1977. On November 18, 1978, he led over nine hundred men, women and children to commit mass suicide—Ed.

mote outcrop of islands, as far removed from the known world as Earth is from Mars, a handful of human beings was encouraged to shoot, club, knife, strangle, drown, or behead one hundred and twenty men, women, and children in a fourteen-week period.

How could this occur? Mainly because one man, Jeronimous Cornelius (quite correctly labeled an aggressive-charismatic by Futcher in *Famous Australian Murders*) was able to so bewitch his followers that they behaved in a manner only equaled in this century by certain Nazi war criminals.

On these tiny islands of coral and rock, Cornelius gave himself the title of Captain General, ruling as a god. And why not? Who had the power to stop him? He was the senior surviving officer of the Dutch East India Company, young, intelligent, and preaching that those who followed his dreadful and selfish schemes could expect the realization of any desire. No doubt, to certain ignorant sailors and soldiers, this was an opportunity not to be missed; to some of the teenage boys—and there were more than thirty deck boys, cabin boys, and cadets aboard the *Batavia*—Cornelius must have sounded like the Pied Piper.

Jan Pelgrom was the classic disciple—unstable, impressionable, and vulnerable.

Of course, it might be argued that since Cornelius had so much power, this somehow excused the murders committed by Pelgrom or by the other murderer whose life was spared, the soldier Wouter Loos. In a modern court of law, such persons could claim temporary insanity because Cornelius had led them astray. They could claim diminished responsibility because they were shipwrecked and under stress, being away from the social and physical comforts of home. They could even claim self defense, arguing that they had killed to protect themselves when faced with a dog-eat-dog struggle for survival.

While anything is possible in court, it's doubtful that a judge would pat Pelgrom on the head, saying "Poor misguided boy" and release him upon the world. Certainly, there is no evidence to prove that this boy was a psychopath, yet it is difficult to disagree with Max Futcher when he states "there is something truly frightful about the character of Jan Pelgrom."

Again we should ask, why was Pelgrom permitted to live?

Perhaps the answer lies with Wouter Loos. Although convicted of murder and fully expecting to die, as did Cornelius and the others, Loos was reprieved at the last moment. Francisco Pelsaert, Commandeur aboard the *Batavia* and later acting as president of the inquiry into the murders, deliberately granted Loos the privilege of life—even though this meant he was to be cast away in a tiny boat with Jan Pelgrom for company.

Why then was Wouter Loos spared? And why was he selected to accompany Pelgrom? There were plenty of other killers to choose from. The story of Wouter Loos leaves us with many questions but very few answers. He certainly does not appear to be typical of seventeenth-century soldiers, who were no more than mercenary thugs. He was singled out from the crowd.

From his first days on the shipwreck islands, Loos was chosen by Cornelius as a special favorite. Not as a servant, as Pelgrom had been, but as a dependable, rational adviser. Yet, when ordered by Cornelius to kill the barrel maker, Jan Willemsz, Loos refused, stating it would be against his conscience to do so. This is a remarkable statement coming from a mercenary soldier; it is equally remarkable that

Cornelius allowed the barrel maker—and Loos—to live.

In the records of the trial that have been preserved in Pelsaert's journal, the Commandeur himself notes that, even under torture, Loos would not confess to participating in the murders. It was said that he tended to listen and speak rather than to act.

Although finally convicted on the evidence of survivors of the massacre, Wouter Loos must have displayed sufficient moral fiber to convince Pelsaert that he was a young man worth saving—if only an excuse could be found to allow it. Possibly, at the last moment, Jan Pelgrom provided Pelsaert with the excuse he was looking for.

On the day of execution, the accused were led to a row of gallows erected on one of the islands where the murders had taken place. Before being hanged, each of the killers was taken to a block where a hand was removed, probably with a blow from an ax. So that the victim did not bleed to death, thus escaping the gallows, the blood flow was staunched by plunging the stump of the arm into molten pitch.

Jeronimous Cornelius, on account of his leadership, lost both hands by this method.

Jan Pelgrom was one of the last to be taken. He had witnessed the deaths of the others and now, in his last moments, overcome by terror and the prospect of hell's yawning mouth, threw himself at the feet of Pelsaert and begged, on the basis of his youth, to be granted life.

There is little doubt that Pelsaert had witnessed enough killing to satisfy even the most ghoulish executioner. Here, in granting this miserable boy's request, he also saw the opportunity to save Wouter Loos.

The pity is that we will never know whether Pelsaert's faith in Wouter Loos was justified. Nor will we ever know if Jan Pelgrom survived to kill again. It would be a frightening possibility . . .

Item 11

Messenger, Midway Roadhouse

I like to sit on my bed going through magazines my mother brings home. I have a good eye for detail. I like looking at pictures of people, not so much famous people but the ones who stand back from the action. In a photo of a crowd, sometimes I see there's a person right at the edge, looking out of the picture.

I have long fingers, thin but strong, and I can move them very precisely to do delicate things. When I was younger I collected stamps and was always careful choosing the right ones and pasting them in squarely. I used a magnifying glass for this purpose, but it was hardly more than a toy, and eventually I picked up another one, more powerful, as I will explain later.

I enjoy working with wire very much. The finer the wire the better, as I weave and knot quite complex shapes. For instance, I made an Eiffel Tower from wire. It's on my bedroom dresser and stands nine inches high. I also made a similar sort of construction, but in reverse (or upside down). This was a funnel web spider's tunnel or trap, but since its narrowest point is at its base (the reverse of the tower, as I said) it was necessary to find something to support or suspend it. I took a Bunsen burner tripod from the science room to do this and now the silvery wire web sits extremely well. It's on my dresser also.

I sometimes think I would be able to do fine handicrafts, such as embroidery or tapestry, but I'm sure I would be laughed at if I did.

At the time of finding the ring I had been experimenting with some heavier gauge wire that Kratz got for me from the Roadhouse garage. Kratz was useful that way. Since my mother came home with trucking magazines mixed among the others, and I had no interest in them, they were traded off to Kratz for anything I wanted that he might happen to have. For example, two or three copies of *Big Rig,* a trucking magazine, was all it usually took to get some good wire.

What I needed at that particular time were ball bearings, maybe about a third of an inch in diameter. I had made this slingshot by braiding the heavy gauge wire through and through. Very strong. I needed the ball bearings as ammunition to fire from it. The Saturday afternoon the instrument was ready for testing, I looked out of my bedroom window to make sure Kratz was messing around at the back of the Roadhouse, then bundled up some magazines to trade.

I never felt good about the garage. It brought out the worst in me. I would move between the fuel drums and old hoists and rusty car bodies, wishing I was invisible or a ghost. And when I found Kratz he never made it easy. Sure, he was happy to trade, but the garage was his little world and he always had to let me know it.

This day he was down the back washing or rinsing some engine part in a metal sink. His hands were covered in thick black grease. I stood behind him, watching, but he must have sensed someone was there and turned around.

Kratz was a bit older than me, nearly seventeen, yet I could look down on him. He was stocky and had thick, nearly black hair. He wore overalls that must have been green once but they were so filthy now they could nearly stand up by themselves. He always had some of the clip buttons undone and I think this was to show there were hairs on his chest. Maybe half a dozen around each nipple. He must have thought that looked good.

He saw me standing there and raised his eyebrows, as if to ask, What do you want?

I said, "I've got some magazines," and he said, "Sure, at what cost?" but he was smiling and his white teeth stood out against the grease on his face.

I told him about the ball bearings. He listened and asked what they were for.

"Ammunition," I said, "for a catapult."

He wanted to know where it was.

"In my bedroom," I said, and he wanted to know why it was there.

I told him I had made it there, out of the heavy wire he got for me. He seemed interested in that, or at least he didn't laugh, and then he asked where I was going to try it. I pointed over the barbed wire to the cliffs. He put down the part he had been rinsing and said he'd see what he could find, then disappeared inside the garage.

I waited around and had a look at what he called his dream machine. This was an old Ford utility pickup truck (maybe 1965 or 66) that had been abandoned on the highway years before. The Roadhouse manager towed it in and dumped it around the back. Nobody ever turned up to claim it so Kratz got permission to do it up. I thought it was a pile of rusted-out junk; to Kratz it was the meaning of life. He reckoned he was going to make it roadworthy and when he got a license he'd head up to North West Cape, to the Satellite Communication Station, where his father was supposed to be a technician. I guessed this was a lie (and I think he knew that) because the Satellite Station was manned exclusively by foreigners, Americans. No locals could get access.

I don't think Kratz had a father at all, but his mother worked in the kitchen at the Roadhouse diner. While my mother brought home papers and magazines, his was always ripping off kitchen leftovers, or so my mother said. She didn't get on with Mrs. Kratzman. Even though they were neighbors for nearly two years, they were never friendly.

It was the same for Kratz and myself. He came over to my place a few times, especially in the beginning when he first arrived, but it didn't work out. He was always touching things in my room, shifting things around. That made me edgy. He stopped coming over after a while. He would still talk to me on the school bus since we had so far to go, or on the long vacations, but not if other kids were around. I didn't feel comfortable with him then. After a while he started spending his time at the garage, and when the dream machine thing got going with the pickup I hardly saw him—except out of my bedroom window, and then I could sit on my bed and watch him anytime, without him even knowing.

I waited around the pickup until he came back. He held out his hand, and in the black hollow of the palm was a shiny metal ball. "Is that okay?" he said. "Is it the right size?"

For a second it lay there, caught by the sun like a little silver-blue earth. Perfect. Then he rolled it into my hand and I nodded.

"There's plenty more," he said. "When are you going to try them?"

"Now," I said, and straight off he asked, "Mind if I come? I'm finished here. I'm ready to drop the engine in and can't find a mechanic who is free to help. I don't suppose you could?"

I shook my head. "You can come," I said, "if you get some more of these ballies. I'll meet you over the wire in five minutes."

There were about 200 yards of red sand and pebbles and low bushes before the cliff edge. Because of the wind, the sand would sting my legs, and the bushes were dry and stunted and bending over, away from the sea. I used to wonder what the place was good for. No one could grow anything there. Nothing productive, anyway.

Kratz was talking all the time we walked, but since the wind was so strong and he was a good bit shorter than me, I kept losing his words. I walked sideways so I could see his lips and hear him better. He was talking about the pickup and how, when the motor was put in, it could be taken for a road test. Body panels were rusted out but the chassis was solid. Once it was running okay and mechanically sound, he would start on the body work, get secondhand parts, rebuild what he had to. Then he said something I couldn't catch because of the wind, and I said "What?" We were nearly at the cliff edge.

He stopped and turned to me. He was yelling. "What color should I paint it?"

I said I didn't know, white maybe, a plain color was always safe. But then he said something very strange.

I think he said, "What color are dreams?" which was a stupid question and I didn't answer it.

We reached the cliff edge and looked down. I had been there plenty of times, but still I always looked down. The drop was nearly sheer, falling about fifty yards to the boiling sea, but in places where even a couple of inches of rock formed a ledge, sea gulls had made their nests. I pointed them out to Kratz. He nodded and I took the slingshot from my back pocket. He put his hand out to take it and I let him. He looked at it, nodding again as if to say it was okay, and returned it. Then, like magic, he produced from somewhere in his overalls a handful of silver balls, maybe eight or nine.

I put one of the ballies in the rubber sling and pulled it back as far as I could and let it go. For a second I thought I saw it arch up, over the sea, then nothing. The wire felt good, very secure, and the release of the rubber was sharp and sudden. I did that again a few times and so did Kratz. Then I thought I'd try for a target.

The gulls were everywhere, not just nesting on the cliff face but wheeling on the wind all around us. I loaded, aimed at one, and fired. Hopeless. Too much wind and a moving target. But the gulls on the cliff were a different matter and I decided to try for them.

I got down on one knee for better stability and leaned forward toward the edge as far as I could. I lifted the slingshot and took a sighting and that seemed all right, so without looking around I put my open hand behind to Kratz, waiting for him to drop a ball into my palm. Nothing happened.

I shook my hand a bit to let him know I was waiting, and just like that I felt something grab me by the wrist and pull me back. I lost balance and fell sideways into the sand. The slingshot dropped out of my hand. Kratz was looking down at me. There was a ring of grease around my wrist where he had grabbed me.

I said, "What's the matter with you?"

Then he knelt down and yelled right in my ear, "No killing."

That's all he said, and next minute he was walking off through the bushes. That was what Kratz was like—always had to make the rules, run the show, be boss. He was moody too.

I thought, "Go! Get lost and good riddance! I was used to being by myself."

I got up, stuck the slingshot in my back pocket, then wandered off to the north where the cliffs jutted out to form a headland. I liked it there.

I remember this particular time very clearly. It makes a vivid picture in my head.

I could get right to the end of the headland, actually sit on the tip of it with the wind pushing into my face and hair. It made me feel like the figurehead on an old sailing ship. It wasn't dangerous. A lump was cut out of the rock and I could get down into it, sort of a cockpit, protected on three sides but open straight ahead. Nobody would ever know I was there. Once I got down I was completely hidden. I was the only one who knew about this. It was a very special place.

That day was fine and clear. If I looked straight down, there were sharks. I could see a school every so often. I have seen dolphins chasing sharks from there too. Turtles were easy to pick out because they were round and slow.

Once I saw a dugong. These are called sea cows. They are like seals but bigger. In a nature magazine they said dugongs were the basis of the mermaid legends for sailors. When the dugong mother feeds her young she lies on her side on the surface and the baby is next to her. I suppose that could look like a woman, or the dead body of a woman, if I saw it from a distance, or from directly above, as the sea eagles would, from the white glare of the sun.

If I looked straight out I could see the horizon curved in a giant arc. Sometimes I could see ships, but if there were, they never seemed to be on the water. They always seemed to be floating above the surface. Suspended in air . . . or space. I could never figure that out.

The wind blew hard against my chest, but I felt the warmth there, beneath my shirt. I put my hands up, undid the leather, and slipped the ring into my palm. Perfect. Golden against the skin.

Holding it to my eye, I could see the ocean framed in a single circle.

Every night now, there were dreams as clear as the picture I could see here. I would go to sleep as usual and the other Steven Messenger would appear, cool in his T-shirt and jeans. As plain as day he would stand by the highway outside the Roadhouse. There was the motel sign flashing VACANCY. Messenger would wait, listening for a sound from the distance. Over the wires maybe, or on the wind from the sea.

Then the craft would come. A circle of pure gold, hovering, and he would look up into white light.

But nothing ever happened—except sometimes there was blood on the highway and I would wake up screaming, leaving the other me out there alone.

I looked at the ring in my hand. The stone was like blood, like a drop of bright blood squeezed from a pricked finger.

I knew I would give anything to be in that dream, and lifted up. I wanted to be out of the blood, safe, inside the white light of the ring.

Item 12

From the Standard, *June 17, 1986*

Murderer's Journal:
Publication Rights Granted

Canberra, Thursday. In an unprecedented move the Commonwealth government yesterday granted the *Standard* exclusive rights to publish the journal of castaway *Batavia* murderer, Wouter Loos.

Speaking at a press conference in the federal capital, the National Heritage minister, Dean Russell, announced the granting of the $40,000 publication rights to the *Standard* on condition that the newspaper publish the Wouter Loos journal within the next month. Since the completion of its translation by Professor Hans Freudenberg of the Australian National University, the journal was offered to the media for publication by contract.

Russell stated that the significance of the discovery was so great that no individual claimant should have entitlement to the document. He dismissed as "foolish" an earlier suggestion by Hope Michaels, director of the Western Australian Institute of Maritime Archaeology, that the journal could possibly be claimed by "the person who found it, or even by the state where it was found."

In response to the statement that the Netherlands government may also have a claim, since the journal's author had been Dutch, Russell stated that to return the document to the Netherlands would be as ridiculous as the British Museum giving the Elgin Marbles back to Greece. "The Dutch can make all the claims they like. The document remains in this country," he said.

The publication fee will be used by the National Heritage Trust to construct suitable museum display facilities for the Loos journal and other items found with it, the so-called cannibal pot and a mummified human hand.

Professor Freudenberg also attended the conference but was unable to disclose details of the journal's contents because of strict copyright regulations. However, he later stated on national television, "There is a very good chance the journal will explain the origin of the hand."

The *Standard* will print the journal in several installments in its weekend edition. No specific date of publication has been fixed.

Item 13

Letter from Dr. Michaels, Tuesday, June 24, 1986

Dear Steven,

No doubt you will be surprised to receive this letter from me, but the truth is that I have good reason to think of you often. You see, on the bulletin board directly above my desk, I have a photograph of you standing at the entrance to the cliff cave. Sergeant Norman sent it for my records. When my secretary saw it she said you were the image of James Dean, the actor. I'm not sure about that, but it is nice to have the picture there as I write. It makes me feel as if I know you.

Well, by this time you should have received from my office a copy of the interim report on the journal of Wouter Loos. I asked my secretary to send you that because, without you, none of this wonderful evidence would have come to light.

I also wanted you to see the report, as I mentioned in it that you might have a claim to the discoveries. Unfortunately, the National Heritage minister, Mr. Russell, has suggested that I had intended to give the discoveries to you. That has been published in the press, and I wanted to clarify that in case you read it and were upset.

I should make it clear that I believe nobody *owns* history. To listen to Mr. Russell, you would think anyone could say history was mine or yours.

You can't treat history as if it were an object you put in a glass case, or hand over to relatives when you die. History is a living thing, changing and growing through each fresh contact with humanity. We are all involved in making history every moment of our lives. I think Mr. Russell would believe *he* could make history because he is the minister for the National Heritage; I doubt that Mr. Russell would believe that *you*, Steven Messenger, a high-school student, could do the same.

Well, I don't agree. The night you lifted the lid from that iron pot it was as if you woke Wouter Loos and Jan Pelgrom from a long sleep. You gave them their lives again. You gave them to us too.

That's what I call making a claim on history, Steven. It's a wonderful, living claim. At least, I expected there would be some official recognition of your part in these discoveries. Some official handing-over of your finds to the relevant authorities. Unfortunately, I seem to be the only person who believes that.

Of course, the investigations are not complete, as there is still the question of the missing ring. I'm looking forward to learning more about that. Maybe the serialization of the journal in the paper will prod someone's conscience enough to get them to return it. What do you think?

Dr. Freudenberg, who translated the journal, has been very quiet about the whole thing, so when it does come out it will be news to me too. But I have my ways and means, and the professor told me the mummified hand was definitely female. What's more, I also know her name. Since the journal will be public in a few days, it probably wouldn't hurt to tell you—her name was Ela. She was a teenager like yourself. I think you have given her a new life too.

Well, Steven, I must go. There is so much to do here. Thank you again for what you have given us—but remember, should you hear anything about that ring, perhaps from some of your friends at school, let me know, won't you?

Regards,
HOPE MICHAELS

Item 14

Messenger, Midway Roadhouse

I have already mentioned that Kratz could be moody and liked to be boss, but the fact was we still had to catch the same bus to school and back every day, and since we lived so far out of Hamelin we were usually the first on and the last off. If everything was okay we would share the back seat. If there was trouble between him and me, or from other kids when they got on, I would stay up the front near the driver.

After the episode with the slingshot (when Kratz yelled at me), I sat up the front. It took two days for him to come down and apologize. He said he was sorry, but he couldn't stand to see living things suffer, like the gulls. To listen to him, you'd think he was talking about the world's rarest bird, like the million-dollar lavender peacock I read about in *Stranger than Fiction*, not the filthy, screeching scavengers that lived on the cliffs.

I didn't say anything like that to him, and next thing he gave me a coil of wire, beautiful and fine, the best ever, and said, "Sit in the back seat."

Kratz was like that—weird—I could never trust him.

But that didn't matter. I didn't want anyone getting too friendly or too close because, since the letter came, I had the feeling that someone knew, or suspected, about the ring. It was the last line: "should you hear anything about that ring, etc., let me know, won't you?"

Very nice and concerned. But I wasn't fooled. Things were happening because of that ring—like how I knew the dead girl's name even before I read about it in the letter. There was no way I was giving that ring back.

The day that letter came I got off the bus after school and went in to pick up the mail from the motel desk (that was our mail box) and went on home.

My mother was still at work so I opened the letter in the front room. I read it a couple of times and couldn't take it in, not there, so I took it up to my place on the headland. Then I read it again.

The bit about me looking like James Dean made me laugh—I had seen pictures of him in movie magazines—and that photo of me outside the cave must have been pretty blurry. But the parts about the ring and the girl's name got me thinking, and I read them over and over.

If I gave that ring up, everything would stop. The letter said history was living, that I was making dead people come alive. But if someone took the ring and put it in a glass case, what would that prove?

I took the leather thong from around my neck. It had gone black with sweat and I didn't like that, but to wear the ring out in the open would be asking for trouble.

Sometimes at night in the dark and dead quiet, I might undo the knot and slip the ring onto the little finger of my right hand. If I held it up to the motel sign, I could see the light inside, throbbing, like a living thing.

Then Steven Messenger would come. He would walk the highway, waiting for the ring to appear, to come down and lift him and carry him away, safe in the white light from its center.

Ela. The letter said the girl's name was Ela. But Steven Messenger had known that, even before the letter came. Since the first night the ring had raised him, or he had let it raise him.

Lifting in a column of white light, he felt the wind in his hair, on his face, against his skin until, angled slightly to the earth, he found himself inside the ring. That's where Steven Messenger found her name.

He reached out to touch the inner walls, gleaming gold, and his fingers felt the word, ELA, scratched there.

But after, by daylight (in what I thought was reality) I could see the same word again on the letter, in my hand. How could he have known, that other Steven Messenger, before the letter told me?

In my secret place, I scraped the ring on the lichen that clung to the rock beside me. Little gray-green tufts, like balls of cottony thread, fell away and were picked up by the wind. With the edge of the ring, I scraped again and again until I had engraved the name clearly in the exposed rock: Ela. The same name as in the ring.

There were other things I saw more clearly too. *He* was the one who looked like a movie star. *He* was the one who stood by the motel sign, thumbs hooked in his jeans, feet apart. Not me. I knew what *I* looked like. I wondered, if he came out by daylight, the other Steven Messenger, would he look like me, dressed in a uniform of nothing-colored school gray, or would he be that other self, the night self, in his T-shirt and jeans? Would he even come by day?

I turned in my secret place, lifting my legs to tuck in neatly. The name on the rock was directly in front of me. I undid the knot in the leather strip and slipped the ring onto my right hand. It fitted my little finger best. Then I closed my eyes, waiting.

There was nothing, not even the feeling of the ring. I counted, like I do if I'm edgy. Ten, twenty, thirty, forty, and at a hundred everything was blank. I thought it was no good and opened my eyes.

Her name was right there, and I lifted the ring hand to touch it. But as I traced the shape of each letter, I sensed from across the sea, far out beyond the sky, that he was coming.

I couldn't make out anything at first, only the curious saucered curve of the distant horizon. Then, as I had often seen ships, a shape appeared, sailing or flying above the surface. Hardly more than a dot. Maybe a sea bird. But as it came closer I knew that this was no bird—a sea bird's flight was never like this. It zigzagged to the left or right, hesitated, then tacked in the opposite direction. It was looking for something, searching. Its altitude varied too—sometimes it hardly cleared the surface of the sea, sometimes it was lost from sight in the glare of the sun.

But it always drew closer until, on the low banking run along the face of the cliffs, I saw its shape clearly.

The sky-ring of the dreams had come.

I saw him, too, and felt ashamed. He was there, in the white light of the center, lying on his stomach, his head resting on his hands, looking down, as if he were supported on glass. In charge, in his movie-star way. And here I was in my uniform, gaping upward like a kid.

The craft moved backward and forward maybe fifty or sixty feet above me. I thought if it came any closer the wind would toss it against the cliff edge. Then it hovered. Stationary. I could see him there, and when he saw me he lifted one hand, signaling for me to come.

I felt myself rise, without any effort, and in a matter of seconds the cliff and sea were far below. I was suspended in space.

The letter and the leather strip from the ring fell out of my lap. They tumbled on the air below me, over and over, in slow motion. I needn't have worried. In that moment the craft took me in, then sweeping down, gathered both objects to itself.

Inside, I turned to look at him, but he was gone. There was only me, dressed in his clothes, seeing with his eyes.

It was night when I left the cliff that time the letter came. The moon was down and there were no stars. Below the cliff face the sea was a black pit. I couldn't tell where earth ended and heaven began—the night joined everything in one.

Groping and stumbling among the bushes, I made my way home along the cliff. But as I turned inland, toward the motel sign, I felt sure someone was there, behind me in the dark.

Item 15

From the Standard Weekend Edition, *Saturday/Sunday, July 19/20, 1986*

A Murderer's Diary
The first installment of the
journal of Wouter Loos

Translated and introduced by Professor Hans Freudenberg.

When the minister for National Heritage engaged me to translate the manuscript that appears for the first time in this paper today, I expected the task would be purely academic. Naturally, I was honored to be undertaking the translation of such an important work and eager to provide as accurate an interpretation of the text as I could, but nothing could have prepared me for the human element, the personality of the writer.

My particular role in the publication of Wouter Loos's journal was to provide a translation of his original Old Dutch text, and to express this in language acceptable to the general public.

Another more literal or academic translation, with annotations explaining my reasons for interpreting certain peculiar Old Dutch words or phrases, will be published in book form at a later date.

As accounts of the *Batavia* disaster and subsequent murders have been well documented by historians—and, more recently, by criminologists—I will not repeat background information here. However, I would like to offer a few words of introduction.

If the journal (or diary, as this newspaper will refer to it) affects you as it has me, your reading will be far more than an interesting peep into the life of a seventeenth-century castaway; this is not some Robinson Crusoe adventure in which the wretched European manages to rise up and conquer yet another unknown and barbaric land for the good of king and country—although it begins that way.

After many painstaking readings of this journal, it appears to me that Wouter Loos was a young man with a great deal to put behind him. While he must have welcomed the chance to be cast away (the alternative was mutilation and hanging), it also seems that he genuinely wanted to atone for his crimes.

For this reason, Wouter Loos's journal begins with a clear note of optimism. He not only intends to survive in this land, he is quite determined to trade with the natives, thereby making his stay worthwhile for the Dutch East India Company. The initial journal entries systematically record Loos's daily activities and future plans. His voice rings out clearly, filled with energy and enthusiasm. But, so like youth itself, this exuberance does not last. Almost imperceptibly, the writer's voice falters; the entries are no longer forward looking or hopeful; any vestige of order is abandoned.

The cause of the change in Wouter Loos—and his narrative—is not difficult to find. Simply expressed, he did not travel alone. From the moment he left the mother ship, Loos was forced into sharing his life with the vilest of creatures, the other castaway, Jan Pelgrom.

Though hardly more than a boy, it was Pelgrom who turned Loos's quest for a new life into a nightmare.

Yet Loos was not the only one to suffer. Those readers who would learn the origin of a young girl's hand, marvelously preserved for over three hundred years, will not be disappointed.

The time has come to share this remarkable journal with you.

This Journal is the writing of Wouter Loos, Aged 24 years,
Soldier of Maastricht who, as a Victim of Fate,
was aboard the *Batavia* when she ran upon
Uncharted Rocks
and, later, again at the Cruel Hand of Fate,
was accused of murder and cast away
on this Unknown Southland. Nov. 16, 1629.
May the Lord have Mercy on my Soul.

Today I begin this journal, it being the first opportunity I have had to do so. Every day I will write, then when I am rescued, those who accused me and yet remain in authority will know that my intentions have at all times been for the good.

Further, I will attempt to be a worthy companion for the boy, Jan Pelgrom, who being spared from death, has been cast away with me and entrusted to my care. Should we be able to trade with the Black Indians who inhabit this coast, as the Commandeur Pelsaert has directed us to do, I fear the boy will be a hindrance. He has no learning, neither can he read nor write. Yet, I will not judge, rather I will thank God that, through His mercy, I am not alone, having with me one of my own kind in this strange land.

There is also a young spaniel pup, born aboard the mother vessel and dropped over the side to us as we pulled away. This little animal, a favorite of the boy, we have named Lucky, in consideration of our present survival.

It is now four days since we were abandoned to make a landing upon this place. The craft in which we were cast adrift was small and unstable, being constructed mainly of timbers from the *Batavia* wreck, and loaded with trade goods. When the line was cast off I was certain we should sink like a mill stone, especially when I looked to shore, a distance of about one mile,[1] and saw the surf beating there. Mercifully, we remained afloat and, gaining confidence in our craft, I did not attempt to land at once but, mounting a small sail, ran North on a calm sea for two days and one night, all the while hoping to sight an opening in the white water through which we could navigate.

In this I was only partly successful. As night fell on the second day, having sighted a break in the surf, I attempted to land. But I had been deceived. The waves I had been watching for so long were breaking on an outer bar of sand, perhaps

---

1. In the seventeenth century, a Dutch mile was the equivalent of approximately 3 English miles—Ed.

five hundred yards from land and, having passed through an opening in this barrier without mishap, I was afraid to see a further line of spray and white water veiling the shore. Into this our craft plunged, and we capsized in a moment.

Of what followed I recall little in particular, save for the boy's screams when first we were tossed and spun about. All seemed to happen at once amid a confusion of senses, until I found myself fighting for life beneath the breakers. It seemed that I had sunk into the darkness of some frightful pit and I struck out, again and again beating with my arms, desperately struggling for air.

I cannot say how long this sensation lasted, but when I felt my life must drain from me, something solid—which I took to be my companion, or the keel of our vessel—struck against my side. At once I reached out, and touching a rope, wound this around my arm. All else was oblivion.

I awoke in the light of morning to find myself washed high upon the beach. Beside me, half buried in the sand and weed, lay a black iron pot, tangled with rope, a length of which remained wound about my wrist. Beyond the pot, facedown on the sand, and likewise caught in the same rope as myself, was the body of the boy.

At once I clambered to my feet, believing him to be dead, but even as I moved, the pup, Lucky, sent up a howling from the sandhills nearby and the boy's eyes opened as I knelt beside him.

I thank the Lord we were saved.

On the morning of the 18th, the boy and I gathered what we could of our belongings. These had been scattered along the beach for a great distance, both to the North and South. Our craft had been split in pieces. We knew then that any hope of return by sea to our own kind would be impossible, but I convinced the boy, who seemed to lose heart at the loss of our craft, that this was all the more reason for us to trade with the Indians. I was certain that if we could find a village or township we would be able to hire or charter a small seaworthy vessel.

Although we salvaged all we could from the beach, many of the trade goods and other personal items that had been given to us were now lost, as indeed was the bulk of our food and water. However, some items stored in small caskets had remained undamaged and we were most grateful that among the casks we found one of water, and several of wine. Until discovering these, we had not drunk for twenty-four hours.

At this time we have camped one night beneath a piece of sailcloth spread over low bushes. It is my intention to remain here until I can sort and dry what has been saved from the sea, then plan our future enterprise. Perhaps as a result of his exposure to the elements, the boy has a fever and is miserable.

November 21, 1629

This is the third day since our landing. I have completed an inventory of our goods, both for trading and personal use:

1. One chest with items for trade:
   40 strings of glass beads (20 red, 20 blue)
   Cloth of fine wool, red and yellow stripes. 10 yards. (Some water damage.)
   20 bone-handled knives.
   4 boxes of looking glasses, 3 × 3 in., unframed.
   6 boxes of iron nails.
   20 disks of bright tin, on ribbon, to give the appearance of insignia of office.

2. One chest of goods:
   1 small ax.

1 small spade.
1 musket, with shot and powder.
1 set of flints with tinder box.
1 burning glass.
2 green glass apothecary jars of ointment.
1 shirt, vest, and breeches each.
1 roll of thread with needles.
1 small cooking pan of iron.
1 journal or logbook.
1 well of ink.
6 fine quills.
(The latter items I now use.)

3. One black iron pot packed with white stockings but containing among these wooden toys from Nüremberg, brightly painted, being figures of soldiers, sailors, villagers, and the like, made to walk with hooks and wires.[2]

4. Bags and containers of victuals (some damaged):
1 cheese.
6 loaves black bread (wet).
26 lbs. of flour (wet).
8 lbs. of salt.
15 lbs. of salt pork.
2 Alters stoneware jugs, sealed, with red wine.
1 water barrel (about 2 gallons).

We have also collected the oak timbers from our craft. These will be put to some use.

Much of the clothing we were wearing at the time of being cast away has been lost. I have my trousers and leather

2. Strange as it may seem, these cheap toys were considered very profitable trade goods. In his ship's log entry for Nov. 16, 1629, Pelsaert specifically mentions supplying these items to the castaways for trade purposes—Ed.

belt, shirt, and vest, one stocking but no shoes, and a hat. The hat I have given to the boy. He is very fair of skin, with pale eyes. His hair is so white and fine, it is like silk. Already from his life on the wreck islands, the heat of the sun has burst the skin, leaving open sores upon his face and hands. Flies settle on these and he is often beating them off. I have applied ointment to the sores. Also his eyes are swollen and he can hardly see because of the sun's brightness on the sand. He is not strong, and often complaining of poor health. Apart from these miseries, the boy has been fortunate to keep his trousers and belt, his shirt, and both shoes.

Our camp has a carnival spirit about it. We have made a fire around which the boy leaps with the pup. The sailcloth from our vessel forms a tent and about all this, spread up and down over bushes, are the bright lengths of fine wool, in red and yellow, which I have unrolled to dry.

It is afternoon now and I will leave shortly to explore in the hope of finding a farm or village.

November 22, 1629

I have searched the land beyond the shoreline sandhills but can find no sign of human life. These appeared to be tracks made in the sand, but no lanes or roads, fences, hedges, or stiles to allow for transport or to separate property from property.

It is very hot away from the sea. Inland the sandhills block the wind and there is no water.

I have gone out alone twice, but found nothing. Tomorrow I will go farther. Perhaps these sandhills are only a barrier that divides the sea from the good land and its inhabitants, farther to the East.

November 23, 1629

When I returned from my travels today, the boy and the pup

had left the camp and were on the beach. In their absence an animal had attacked our flour supply, eating through the bag and spreading and soiling what was not eaten. This is a great loss, as the little I could salvage by scraping it from the earth was fouled with grit and twigs.

Our water is also very low, barely a gallon. I have found none to add to this, neither from a well or a stream.

November 24, 1629

Today I instructed the boy to remain at camp, guarding our supplies. He is becoming sullen. If it were not for the pup, I believe he would be worse.

My exploration has again proved a failure, but climbing some higher dunes to the North, I saw what appeared to be a row of larger trees, perhaps four miles from our camp. We must move in that direction tomorrow.

I regret the boy does not take measures to conserve our supplies. At camp is now only half a gallon of water.

November 25, 1629

This has been a day of great rewards and I thank God. Rising early, I woke the boy and sought his help to construct a means of moving our goods North to the patch of trees I had seen in the distance.

During the night when I could not sleep it had come to me how alike these sandhills were to our hills under winter snow at home. With this thought I planned a means of constructing a sled. We had salvaged several oaken pieces that had formed the keel timbers of our unfortunate landing craft. Two of these could be used as runners beneath the sled, while others might be nailed across the runners to form a base or platform upon which our goods could be stacked. The wide bench seats from our craft, of which I had found two, I might fix to form a high back, so that the sled may either be pushed from behind, or pulled by ropes attached to the front.

While the task seemed simple, the process of construction did not prove to be so. The oak was heavy and hard as iron. As we had no means of sawing the timber, having only an ax with which to work, I was forced to use whole pieces, irregular in shape as they were, and in handling these I required the boy's assistance. He was not a willing worker; in fact his constant disappearances added to my labor as I was obliged to seek him out, either from the sailcloth shelter or the beach, where he would be found foolishly playing with the pup. For these absences he blames his health, and indeed, he does not look well.

Nonetheless, despite this distraction and my limited supply of tools, by mid-morning the sled was complete. With a feeling of great satisfaction I loaded our goods upon it, covering all with the sailcloth that had been our shelter.

As we were about to leave, my companion came running from the bushes carrying a long straight stick, the flower spike of the curious grass trees that spring up from the sand on stems like the mushrooms of home. This stick he wedged among the supplies, so that it stood upright, as a mast, and to this he tied one of the many white stockings we had found in the iron pot.

"Now," he said, "we have a flag to march under," and with that flimsy emblem of our mission waving above us, we made our way to the beach; myself in harness, dragging the sled, while the boy and his pup capered in circles round about.

I could not help but wonder what the inhabitants of the land would think should they have seen us, but later, when we had traveled about two miles, and not come across so much as a sign of humanity, I began to doubt that this place was inhabited at all, and considered it rather as the barren face of the distant moon, empty of life, and we the first persons who had trodden upon it.

So I passed most of the day, dragging the sled upon the sea shore. If this was covered in stones from a rocky outcrop, I turned up into the bordering sandhills and towed my burden there. The heat was very great and the boy's complaints of thirst were constant. At first I stopped to tend to these, allowing him sips of our remaining water, of which we had little more than a quart, until at length I ignored him, as he did nothing to help or otherwise earn his reward, and I feared that unless I pressed on, we would die of thirst before reaching our shaded destination.

Later in the day, I was pleased to find a remarkable lake, where the sandhills ended. Yet, this is indeed a strange land, for the water of the lake was like nothing on this earth, being of a rose color, and not fresh, but thick with salt.[3]

Beyond the lake, we arrived at a point where the sand had been deeply channeled by water running off the land. These channels were dry, but it was evident that a torrent of water had passed here, and I concluded that inland, no great distance, a dam or water gate had burst, causing this destruction.

As the boy was moaning and set to fall down in a faint, I took the water and left him with the sled while I followed the channels inland to locate their possible origin, presuming this would be a mill or irrigated field.

In this search I was disappointed. I had left the boy hardly twenty minutes and proceeded inland, when the deep

---

3. This clearly establishes the landing in the vicinity of the Hutt Lagoon, where the water has a distinctive pink color, due to the natural occurrence of beta carotene, which is mined today for use as a food coloring—Ed.

channels disappeared, and a great floodway opened before me, its dry, sandy bed covered with rocks and the dead trunks of many trees.[4] The steep banks were dotted with trees also, and I had no doubt that these were what I had seen from our earlier camp in the South. It appeared to me that this vast and open area, gouged from the earth, was the result of a mighty disaster, but having walked on for almost an hour, I could find no evidence of its cause, or any form of human habitation.

Knowing that the boy would be fearful in my absence, and aware that night was near, I stumbled back down the floodway toward the sea. It was then that I saw a flock of white cranes rise from beside a mound of rocks in the middle of the stony bed and, knowing that in the Lowlands of my home these birds fed by water, I turned to the spot where they had been.

I was quite correct in my guess, for here, protected from the burning sun by the shadow of the rocks, lay a small pond. The water's edge was muddied and the surface green with slime, but being overcome by thirst I fell on my knees to drink.

As I leaned forward the slime was broken by an upheaval from beneath and I leapt back, thinking some creature or water sprite lurked in the depths. Then I saw the cause of my fear: nothing more than fish, many of good size, flopping about in the shallow water that hardly covered their bodies, streaked green and gray by the clinging slime.

I was glad no one had been about to witness the foolishness of my reaction and, recovering myself, I cleared away some of the scum, then managed to scoop several handfuls of the muddy water to my parched lips. The taste was very

4. Probably the dry channel of the Hutt River—Ed.

strong and the liquid coated my mouth with a thick, greasy lining of slime, but I was refreshed nonetheless.

My thoughts returned to the boy and I determined to fetch him to this place at once. Certainly the water and fish would be of great benefit to our failing supplies, but also, I might use the spot as a base to explore the dry bed further, in the hope of locating the Indians, if indeed there be any in this land.

And so it is that I finish this day's entry. We have camped on the bank high above the pond. Our sailcloth is spread between giant trees and, beside a good fire, the boy picks at the bones of fish I scooped from the water with my bare hands. The pup, Lucky, is also content, being curled in a deep sleep upon the lid of the iron pot.

November 26, 1629

I have traveled far up the floodway and found nothing. On my return I followed the top of the bank, searching all the while for food or signs of habitation, but with no success. There are low, dry bushes, but no berries, herbs, or sweet grasses that can be used for food. There are few trees, and even these bear no fruit. They may be of value for building, being of great height, straight and limbless, but as there are no forests, it is doubtful that the timber cutter could find enough to fell. In the great heat the trees shed their bark, even as the sun has stripped us of our skin.

On my return to camp tonight we again dined on fish from the pond. I have checked our remaining stores and found them in poor condition, the heat having caused some items to putrefy.

We have remaining:

2 loaves of black bread.
1–2 lbs. of flour (soiled with sand and sticks),

4 lbs. of pork, which cannot last much longer.

Some salt.

1 jug of red wine.

Our stored water is now all used. I have taken the empty cask to the pond and here I gather the mud in a stocking, then squeeze it through the fabric. Thus some water is strained and gathered. This is a slow process and I doubt it can be continued for long.

Even in the two days we have been here, the pond has withered, and the few fish that remain cannot supply our needs for more than another day. Tomorrow I must find supplies or other human beings, else we will surely perish.

November 27, 1629

Again I searched high above the floodway, this time to the North. Nothing was found. I begin to believe that there was no dam burst in this place, but perhaps it is a dry riverbed that runs only in season, and my searching for signs of human endeavor is to no avail.

Today I went farther inland than I have been before, leaving early, and returning at dusk. While I found no signs of human life, I was fortunate to discover the recently dead carcass of a small animal in the riverbed. This creature has the appearance of a large rat, with small front paws but long stronger rear legs, as a dog. It has a thick tail and is covered overall in brown fur. The face is soft, with the eyes of a calf.

The animal appeared to have fallen among the stones, for its legs were twisted beneath its body. This creature I dragged back to our camp, where it was immediately skinned by the boy and prepared for roasting.

The blood of the animal we have mixed with flour for a fine black pudding.

November 28, 1629

We have lived off the dead animal last night and today. Though our water supply is all but gone, I have not left camp.

November 29, 1629

Hopeless search for food or water.

November 30, 1629

Again searched for water and returned to camp late. The boy is of no help, spending his day lying beneath the sailcloth cover, complaining and moaning. He has lost interest in the pup, which spends most of its day in the cool mud of the pond. The flies and heat are unbearable. I have not the energy to attend to the boy's needs and I endeavor to ignore him.

December 1, 1629

It is now sixteen days since we were left by the mother ship and I fear our lives are lost. We have no supplies, but for a few mouthfuls of wine. The boy remains alive by filling his mouth with mud from the pond.

December 2, 1629

This day I had taken what was left of the wine and returned to the beach to search for shell fish or crabs that may have been washed up there. By midday I had found nothing, and was returning to camp when I caught the smell of flesh roasting.

Presuming the boy had captured some game, I hurried to him but as I stumbled through the low bushes into camp, I saw what he had done. Lucky, the unfortunate pup, had been spitted over the fire, and crouching there, waiting to devour this awful meal, was my hateful companion. Seeing me appear so suddenly, the boy was at first overcome with shock, then gathering his senses, he became bold, taking up the ax and challenging me in thick and garbled speech that, should

I touch the carcass, I too would suffer a similar fate.

From the contortions of his face and the madness in his pale eyes, I had no doubt that he told the truth.

Sickened, I have left him to his meal and withdrawn under the sailcloth. I will keep the musket with me at all times. He eats furtively, with the ax beside him. So it has come to this. Tonight I will take fire down to the pond and squeeze out the mud which remains there. In the morning, whether he comes with me or not, I will take the sled and head North along the beach. Should I die, it is the will of God.

This concludes the first installment of the Loos journal.

Item 16

Extract from a Letter to the Editor, the Standard,
Wednesday, July 23, 1986

. . . Professor Freudenberg has no doubt accomplished a major task in translating the Loos journal from the original old Dutch; it seems such a pity that so eminent a scholar should be such a poor judge of human nature.

Is the good professor quite serious when he writes in his introduction to the Loos journal of the "human element, the personality of the writer"? If he is serious, then does he expect other readers will also be charmed (or is it fooled?) by the honeyed tones of its author?

Really, Professor! The man who you claim "had a great deal to put behind him" was a murderer and a rapist, tried and sentenced for his crimes. There is little doubt in this reader's mind that the same persuasive skills Loos employed to escape the gallows would be used again to make himself sound noble when he writes of his exploits in his journal.

Reconsider his motives for keeping such a record in the first place, quoted here in his own words:

> Every day I will write, then when I am rescued, those who accused me . . . will know that my intentions have at all times been for the good.

What would he be expected to say: "I will keep this journal to prove I am no better than an animal"?

No, Professor. Here is one reader who remains unconvinced.

Skeptic
Melbourne

Item 17

Messenger, Midway Roadhouse

I remember the time a client suicided in one of the motel rooms, slashed his wrists in the shower and bled to death on the bed. Kratz got to know about that well before Sergeant Norman or the ambulance arrived. I happened to be in the Roadhouse Cafe (getting a Coke) when he came in and told me the body was there, and in which room. I had never seen a dead body.

Around the back of the motel were places where I knew the mechanics went to spy. There were places where they got down on their hands and knees and pressed one eye up to the motel wall, looking inside. I had watched them doing that from my window.

I wondered if I went around the back myself, whether I

would be able to look in and see the body. Of course I didn't, as that would have been disgusting, although later Kratz did give me a description, and it was like I could see it all. But that's what started me thinking. I wondered what Kratz knew about me . . . if he watched me too . . . if he was the one behind me that night on the cliffs.

It wasn't that I actually distrusted Kratz, it was just that I valued my privacy. The last thing I wanted was for someone like him to find out I had the ring. Or worse, what I had learned about it. How I could call it down. How it could show me what no one else had ever seen—or was ever likely to see either, if I had my way.

After school, up at my place on the headland, or even at night in bed (it didn't matter so long as I was alone) I could slip the ring on my finger, close my eyes, and wait. At first he would always be there, the other Steven Messenger, with his movie star pose, but after a while I would only see him sometimes at night, standing under the motel sign. And not so often. He might even have been my imagination. It depended on how the light from the bed lamp hit my window, how the light was refracted from the glass.

Sometimes I just saw myself. Maybe not so cool, but I didn't care. What really mattered was that when I had the ring on I would be lifted up and taken away.

At first I could only see the highway, a thin line going off into the distance both ways. Then when I was more used to things I could go out over the desert, or cross the cliff edge over the sea. That was good for a while. But you get bored if you do the same thing all the time.

The best part was, when I wanted more, the ring seemed to know. I had found that out one night lying in bed, staring out the window. The ring was on my finger, but I wasn't thinking about it, I was thinking about the dead girl, Ela—

about who she really was and where she came from. Then everything changed without any warning. I wasn't in bed anymore but over the sea, looking down from the clear blue of a midday sky. Below me something was floating, a square shape, and as I hovered this grew clearer, until I could pick out every detail.

On the surface was a raft, quite still, and the tiny figure on it seemed to be dead. There was no breeze, not the slightest breath, and the heat was terrible.

But something was alive. From the shadow of a drooping sail a girl appeared, all in white, crawling over the gaping planks. Her shapeless clothes showed the thinness of her body. Long yellow hair tumbled down her back and fell across her face, keeping it from the burning sun.

There were three others on that raft, all dressed in white like the girl. One was a woman. She lay on her back, her eyes wide open, staring into the sun. A baby was in the crook of her arm, its head on her exposed breast. They were both dead.

The other person was a boy, about five or maybe six years old. The girl had crawled over to him. She knelt beside him and lifted his head to her lap, stroking his hair, yellow like hers, and bent toward his face as if she was speaking. Then she lifted her head to the sky.

I pulled back, sure she would see me.

She was looking up as if she could see past the clouds or the sun, straight into heaven itself. Or even beyond that. As if she could see something no one else would ever see or know. Her eyes were clear blue, her skin was very fair, the shape of her face was perfect. She was the most amazing person I have ever seen. I knew for sure she was Ela, and that the ring belonged to her.

She looked down and spoke to the boy again then, lifting him from behind, pulled him back into the shade of the sail where I couldn't quite see. But not for long. Soon she reappeared, again on her hands and knees, and made her way in the direction of the woman and baby. She reached out to touch the woman's face, and without any hesitation, in a single movement of her hand, closed the lids of the dead eyes. She knelt for a few minutes, one hand resting on the mother's head, the other on the baby's, then, showing terrific strength, she dragged the bodies (still in each other's arms) toward the edge of the raft. Here she stopped, looked up again at the sky, and eased both bodies into the sea.

The girl would never know what came next. Although she stayed at the edge of the raft, watching the bodies float there, she could not have seen what I did from above, looking directly down as I was.

The mother's hair spread out and floated about her in a circle of gold and, with the baby still cradled in the protection of her arm, she made an unforgettable picture. A real scoop for a magazine. But it only lasted a minute, then the bodies sank.

Seeing all of this was like looking into somebody else's life. I wouldn't want that to happen to me, but I couldn't do anything to help the girl and it wasn't as if I could speak to her or cheer her up. Besides, I wanted to see more.

That's when I started going up to the headland all the time. Too often, maybe. It turned out to be a stupid thing to do. But for a while I was left alone and, every time, the ring showed me more and more.

Ela's raft seemed to be a piece of ship's decking—gray, splintered planks, maybe twelve feet square. It didn't actually float on the surface, but slightly beneath it, so that a constant movement of pale water washed backward and forward, and lumps of stringy seaweed were tangled around a makeshift mast. From this hung a weathered sail but, since there was no wind, she used it as protection for herself and the boy. When she was in the shade her long yellow hair was knotted at the back. Beside the mast was a chest, like a treasure chest, and from that she would offer the boy a drink out of a flask or canteen. I could see he could barely take sips.

I had been close enough to see her lips move, to know she was speaking, but one afternoon I also actually heard her voice. At first I couldn't make out a thing. Her language sounded like a record that's played at a slower speed. Not that the words came slowly, they didn't, and it wasn't as if her speech was slurred either. The problem was I seemed to recognize the sounds she was making (I could almost understand the words), but not exactly.

It took quite a while to solve the language thing. I kept going back to the same scene, over a few afternoons and nights, as if I were winding and rewinding a tape to get the missing words of a song. But I did it. I concentrated on that single picture of her giving the boy water and, one night (or in the early hours of the morning), I understood her saying "more." Then I picked up the line, "a little more," because she offered him the flask again, and after that there was no problem. Well, not for me, anyway. But the boy was in real trouble. His lips were thick and cracked and his mouth was gaping open so I could see the swollen tongue, like a lizard's on the hot rocks above the cliffs. The skin had peeled almost completely from his face, which was red raw from exposure.

Ela kept his head in her lap. Her long hair protected her from the sun but, when she looked up, it was plain that she was messed up too. Her face had puffed, losing its shape, and her eyes were narrow slits.

She would say to him, "Harry, you have to drink. Harry, you have to." But the boy didn't show any sign that he would drink, or even that he heard. She sipped from the flask herself and put it back in the chest.

Another time I saw them, there was no sail and the chest had gone. Ela was sitting in a corner of the raft, and the boy Harry was lying on his back. As usual his head was in her lap, but her hair was down, and she had spread it like a tent to cover him. She was looking straight out, never up, so I could not see her face. The raft was moving in a circle. It wasn't going anywhere. From where I was, I could see that, but I'm sure she knew it too.

The last time I saw Ela, that is, before everything got messed up, was on the headland one Saturday afternoon. I could see that the raft was inside a reef, in shallow water, maybe a hundred yards off a sandy beach. There were no waves; the surf was breaking farther out. In this little cove the water was very calm. Harry was lying on the raft, like he did, but for a minute I couldn't see Ela anywhere. Then she appeared in the water behind the raft, pushing it toward the shore. All the while she pushed, I could hear her speaking.

"We are safe now. I told you we would be safe," and other things like that.

When they beached, Ela came ashore and dropped to the sand. She stayed there, facedown. After a while she got up and walked first to the south, then north, and above the sandhills. But there was nothing anywhere, no shade or water. From high up I could see that. There was nothing for maybe six miles either way.

She went back to the raft and sat on the sand beside Harry. She started to talk. Her speech was soft and I couldn't get most of what she was saying, but certainly it made no difference to him. When I came down closer, to pick up her voice better, I could see he was dead, but she kept on as if he were listening.

"I will make a bed for you," she said. "You can rest there out of the sun until I fetch help."

All the while she stroked his hair. I could tell she was wasting her time.

At the base of the sandhills she dug his grave, lining it with dry seaweed collected from above the tide line. When this was done she dragged him from the raft, up the beach, and settled his body on the bed of weed. Then she did a very strange thing. Bending forward, she pulled her dress over her head and stood naked. She did this so quickly I was not prepared. I could not believe what I was seeing.

This girl was red and white. While the private parts of her body that had been covered were pure white, her face and arms and legs right to the feet were bright red. I was amazed, and watched very closely.

She tore a piece of material from her dress and placed it neatly over Harry's upturned face. Now, kneeling beside him, she pushed the sand gently over his body, working upward from his feet. His face was covered last. Then she dressed herself.

I could have said something to her, I was close enough, right beside her. But I didn't. It wouldn't have done any good.

I moved in front of her, watching her hands pat down the sand. I think it was then that things started to go sour on me. Most things have a beginning, some specific time when they spin off on a life of their own. And watching her hands there, with the sand between her fingers, was the start of something for me.

For the first time I noticed there was no ring. Of course I had thought it was hers, that it would be there on her finger where I could see it plainly. But it wasn't. Nor was it around her neck. Nor on the bare planks of the raft, already washed by the first waves of an incoming tide.

I pulled myself out of the picture and looked at the ring on my finger. If Ela didn't own it, who the hell did? I could guess by this time how she came to be there—from a wreck at some time or other—and that she was English. I knew that from her speech, even though it was different from mine. But the ring had me fooled. I thought it had been in that iron pot maybe for centuries, right there on her dead hand, just waiting for me to warm it up, give it life.

I touched her name where I had scraped it on the rocks.

That's when my heart stopped—for sure, someone else had been here. Right beside the letters I had made were other marks, scratched clearly in the rock. They formed the shape of a human hand.

Item 18

From the Standard Weekend Edition,
Saturday/Sunday, July 26/27, 1986

A Murderer's Diary
The second installment of the
journal of Wouter Loos.

Translated and introduced by Professor Hans Freudenberg.

In presenting this second extract from the Loos journal, it seems necessary to make mention of the numerous letters to the editor commenting upon the aspects of the initial journal entries.

Many of these letters questioned my sympathy for the writer, Wouter Loos, and stated that his language had fooled or charmed me into believing he was a true and noble soul.

Might I suggest that the readers who made such claims would do well to read my introduction again, in particular the following: "nothing could have prepared me for the *human* element, the personality of the writer."

This is not an admission that I think Loos's behavior was at all times worthy and admirable. I would presume that he ran with the other murderous thugs following the *Batavia* wreck, but here, in the journal under consideration, it is neither his badness nor goodness that concerns me; it is his humanity, his involvement in the business of living, in sharing the hopes and fears experienced by all of us, irrespective of personal past or present circumstances.

Besides, if judgments must be made, surely it is better to wait until the whole tale has been told—if, of course, that will ever be.

The following undated journal entries apparently cover the nights of December 2 to December 4, 1629. For reasons which become clearer later, they have no doubt been written at a later date, probably during the period from December 4 to December 16.

Never will I doubt that there is a God in heaven, or that He looks down upon and cares for me.

Again and again I have stumbled to the very edge of death, and yet at the last moment, He has caught me up and led me to safety.

So it was when the vessel *Batavia* tore itself to pieces upon rocks and I found my way to an island.

So it was when I was led with the murderers to be hanged that the Commandeur offered me life upon this Southland.

So it was when landing here that our craft was capsized but I was caught up by the iron pot and carried to shore.

And now, when I was certain I would perish of starvation or thirst, or be murdered by the ax of the boy Pelgrom, once more I have been granted life.

It has been some days since last I wrote and much has taken place that I must record. I *will* have it known that in all things I have acted for the good.

The night following the death of the pup, I spent mostly in the bed of the dry river, wringing from the mud pool what little filthy water it would yield and collecting this in one of the empty wine vessels. The boy did not attempt to join me but remained on top of the river bank, occasionally appearing with the ax and shouting frightful threats that I would soon become his nourishment, as surely as the unfortunate pup.

I admit these threats filled me with terror, and never at any time did I consider them to be false. Throughout the night I kept the musket beside me, and went about my task by the light of a great fire.

At first light I took what water had been collected, about two quarts, and, heading up the riverbed, climbed the bank at a point out of sight of my companion, then skirted back through the low shrubs to approach him from behind. As I hoped, he was sound asleep, the meal he had made of the pup no doubt giving him the contentment of a full belly, but the ax remained gripped in his thin fingers.

I stood still, watching him. One shot from the musket neatly placed through his skull would have ended my troubles with him, but I had seen enough killing on the islands and put the thought from my head. Around the fire were scattered the remains of the pup, picked clean and covered in ants. I wondered if I had been a fool, that the death of the pup was not important, possibly something we would have had to do anyway. And I could have bent down then and woken the boy, to ask forgiveness. He was, after all, my sole companion.

I moved a few steps toward him, and in doing so, felt a light tug against my foot. At once, I realized the foolishness of my trust. The area about him was crisscrossed with fine threads (drawn no doubt from the bolt of wool) and several of these had been knotted to the handle of the ax. This was a snare, carefully constructed to warn him of my approach. All this I saw in a moment, and no sooner had I understood the situation than the boy was standing before me, barely awake, but in his eyes was the same madness I had seen the day before.

Gripping the ax, he circled around me, gabbling in his thick voice that I would soon be cut to pieces, that he would boil my flesh in the iron pot, and other obscenities that I will not mention here for fear of disbelief. All this he did while I held the musket upon him, but his face was frightful, and the gleam of teeth over his swollen lips was terrible to behold. I am not a weak man, being strong of limb though short, yet this bloodless boy, pale and lank as he may be, filled my heart with terror.

I was taken with the urge to fire the musket and be done with him. There was no chance of missing, as my range was hardly a yard and he would be dead at my feet before the ax could fall.

But I could not fire, and began to call out above his voice, shouting wild and rash promises of rich and well-watered lands I had seen beyond the river, a paradise waiting for us if only he would go with me a little farther.

At last he seemed to listen, and I lowered the gun as a sign of peace, at the same time moving backward to brace myself against the sled. I asked him to come with me one more day—telling him I had water—then should we find nothing, he could do with me as he wished, eat me alive should he so desire and I would not resist, for I would be beyond caring.

Not for a moment do I think he believed a word I said, but he lowered the ax and turned away, kicking the earth in barely contained fury and uttering curses against God and man.

For some time I leaned against the sled and watched him. He seemed to have forgotten me and moved off a little, out of my sight among the low bushes of the river bank. Presently I heard him vomiting, and took it that the flesh of the pup had been too much for his nearly empty stomach. I was sorry to think that poor Lucky's death had brought so little advantage.

When the sled was fully packed I took down the sail-cloth sheet and once again used it to cover our load. Then I called for the boy. At first I thought he would not come, but presently he emerged from the bushes, looking as if he would fall dead at any moment. The ax was still in his hand.

"I am going," I said. "I will head North."

He seemed to pay me no attention at all, but stood where he was, in the clearing near the remains of the fire.

"Are you coming?" I said. But again there was no response.

I had tired of his ways and, without hesitation, I slipped into the harness of the sled and moved off toward the sea.

I do not know when he moved, but by the time I had proceeded some distance up the beach I looked back to see him following, although not with any conviction, and apparently more out of the notion that there was nothing else to do.

During the whole of that day I dragged the sled upon a smooth and sandy beach, stopping at times to sip the water, or sit briefly in the narrow shade cast by the load. At such times the boy would stop too, but he never attempted to join me. Rather he would feign some distraction, such as a sudden interest in a shell or the weed at the tideline, or he would simply sit among the ever-present sandhills. He was clearly unwell, but the ax never left his hands.

By evening I had again begun to despair. The landscape had not changed nor had there been any sign of human habitation or industry—not a boat, or dock, or seaside tavern. There was nothing.

My water could last perhaps one more day, but I was most in fear of the night, and the dreadful promise I had given the boy.

By dusk I was almost ready to meet my God. Through the long afternoon I had made my peace with Him many times over, and now, as the sun began to dip, I determined to proceed to a distant outcrop of bushes rising from the sandhills, check these for any sign of life, then fall upon the mercy of the boy.

As the expectation of death was foremost in my brain, I was certain a sudden burst of frightful shouts behind me meant that he was closing for the kill, and in prayerful resignation I fell to my knees in the sand.

Although I waited, the screaming grew no closer, and lifting my head, I turned to see the cause of the uproar.

The boy was in fact quite far behind, perhaps a hundred yards, standing in the parallel tracks of the sled. I saw the ax at his feet, his hands clasped to his head in an attitude of terror and his gaze directed toward the sandhills above him.

It was then that I first sighted the Black Indians of this Southland.

Three of these persons stood on the ridge of sandhills, staring down upon us. They were nearer to me than the boy, no more than thirty yards behind. At once I felt an awful terror, far greater than that which the boy had provoked in me—for in their hands were great spears, and the fineness of their forms, black against the sky, was terrible to behold. Although I had waited for so long to meet a fellow human, my hand moved at once to the place beneath the sailcloth where I had concealed the musket, for already the Indians had moved toward the beach.

Then fell a sudden quiet. The boy had ceased screaming and now dropped to his knees, even as I had done, no doubt to better accept the termination of his life. But such an act of violence seemed quite foreign to those who had stumbled upon us. Ignoring both myself and the boy, the Indians moved clear of the sandhills and crossed the beach to the sled tracks that marked our progress.

Now here was a curious thing. The long straight tracks of the sled disappearing down the beach, the boy and myself kneeling upon them, and the Indians coming to a sudden halt midway between us. So we remained, as if we were frozen, in that peculiar manner.

The noise of raised voices broke the silence. It was not that the Indians spoke in hostility, rather their tones were light and excited. Nor were their spears used in the demonstration of violence, but to prod and poke the sand where it had been depressed by the weight of the timber runners beneath our sled. This discussion lasted several minutes, after which time the men (for their nakedness made it obvious they were males) trotted quietly South. At this movement the boy set up a most frightful shrieking—considering no doubt that as the Indians moved in his direction, he was about to die— but he was given a wide berth, and some fifty yards beyond him they stopped again, once more dropping to the sand to examine our tracks.

This series of movements was repeated several times at varying distances along the beach to the South when, without so much as a glance at us, the Indians vanished from sight into the sandhills, leaving the boy and myself still kneeling where we had dropped, overcome with terror.

I could not say which of us first took his eyes from the sandhills; perhaps it was simultaneous, but I know there was a time when, without moving, we simply stared at one another, face to face, along the connecting track of the sled.

Then the boy bolted. He first clutched the ax and in a low stumbling run made directly for me. I had not released my grip of the musket, but his expression alone said I would not need it—he was gasping and sniveling with fear, not rage. On reaching the sled he dropped the ax and fell to the sand beside me, clutching at my clothes and pointing toward the sandhills as if I had been entirely unaware of our previous encounter.

"Did you see?" he was gibbering. "Did you see? They will kill us. I know it. Kill us and eat us."

He was too close to me now, pawing at me, and I pushed him off. He was a pathetic creature, and witnessing this display of cowardice was not likely to arouse my sympathy. This was the very brute who but hours before had been prepared to carve me up for his next meal. Now he groveled for protection at my feet.

His weakness was my strength. Regaining my presence of mind, I picked up the ax and slipped it under the covers beside the musket. It was better that both weapons remained out of his sight—I knew from experience how quickly his moods might change. Having done that, I pulled him to his feet and shook him, telling him to act the man at least, although he was hardly more than a child.

"Why should they kill us?" I asked him. "Have we done them any harm?"

His eyes were still wide with terror and he would not look at me, but stared over the load on the sled toward the sandhills, his breathing short and labored.

"They are Indians," he said, "and naked. In the Brazils the naked Indians are the cannibals who live on white flesh."

I could not deny the truth of what he said, and felt my heart sink again. Many was the tale I had heard in a tavern, or aboard ship, of the frightful rites and habits of these Indians. Some gathered white skins, seeking tattoos, others human skulls, while others wanted nothing more than to feast upon the flesh of the white man, which tasted sweet and was favored more highly than pork.

"And their bodies," he said. "You saw how lean and hungry they were."

But I could listen to no more.

"You talk like a fool," I said. "If all this is true, why did they leave us? Surely they could see we were on our knees in terror. You dropped the ax, and I could not use the musket." I regretted having said that, not wanting to remind him of its whereabouts, but he seemed not to care.

"You are the fool," he said. "Did you see how they went around me, checking our tracks to find if there were others like us following? They will keep watch to make certain of our numbers, then they will attack. Even while we talk they will be watching—from up there." He pointed to the sandhills. "Tonight they will come when they are certain we are only two."

As much as I despised him, I knew that there was reason

in what he said. Certainly the Indians had circled him, checking the tracks, and night was almost upon us. But I could not bring myself to agree, or to show my own fear before him, and strove to maintain my attitude of scorn for his ideas. I said we would know soon enough and there was little we could do about it, even if they should come. Rather than quake in fear, we must make full use of the remaining daylight to build a fire and wait to see what happened. I could easily have said, "Be ready when they come," for in my heart I believed they would, and it was better that we were on the beach, forcing them to attack in the open.

So I said, "Here. We will camp where we are," and, slipping the musket into my belt, I moved from the protection of the sled to gather driftwood at the tideline. My actions were greeted with a howl of dismay and the boy leapt after me as if I were abandoning him to die. Again I pushed him back, calling him a fool and a coward, but he would not leave me, and although I made three trips to gather wood, he collected not so much as a single stick, dancing around me jabbering nonsense and casting looks of terror toward the sandhills all the while.

By nightfall I had built a good fire and, with the musket in my lap and the sled between myself and the sea, I prepared to keep watch over the sandhills until dawn. The boy declared he would keep guard with me but, as was his way, he soon fell into a fitful sleep upon the sand.

Throughout that long night the awful crying from his tortured dreams was my greatest source of terror.

When first light showed behind the sandhills, I greeted it in the belief that this would surely be my last day upon the earth—a belief made all the more certain by the appearance of Indians upon the beach, perhaps two hundred yards to the South.

As the sun had not entirely risen above the level of the sandhills, the boy still slept, and thinking it wise under present circumstances to leave him alone, I rose slowly to my feet, still gripping the musket, to face whatever fate might have in store for me.

This time there were seven Indians and, although I could not tell if the three from the previous day were among them, as to me all shared a sameness of appearance, it was clear from the long gray beards of two of their number that they were old men who had been brought to inspect our tracks upon the sand. These they studied with great care, again prodding with spears or kneeling in the sand to inspect them more closely. It seemed to me that the marks of the sled caused the greatest concern, not our footprints, although those of the boy, who still wore his shoes, were touched upon more so than my own bare prints.

Presently, following the tracks toward us, the Indians grew quite near, perhaps fifty yards away, and I could quite plainly hear the high, excited tone of their voices. The boy woke at this, and was about to begin his usual show of sniveling fear when I kicked at him with my foot, indicating that he be quiet. For once he showed some sense, and rose slowly and quietly, his back, like mine, pressed hard against the sled.

His movement either made no impression upon our visitors or went unnoticed, for they continued to talk as before and showed not a sign of hostility.

They were close to us now, no more that fifteen yards away. I could see their bodies, what little clothing they wore, and their terrible spears, quite clearly. Apart from the two old men, who were completely naked and carried no weapons, there were three fine and handsome warriors with short black beards, and two boys, perhaps the same age as the one whose teeth I could hear chattering in my ear. The men and boys each carried a spear and from a girdle of cord about their waists hung a piece of woven fabric to conceal their genitals. Their skin was heavily scarred with weals to form raised and regular patterns. I thought then that such marks could not be the result of random wounding in warfare, but the outcome of some deliberate and terrible tribal ritual. Again my fears of a hideous death came upon me and I tightened my grip upon the musket.

At last they approached us directly. I confess that, in my terror, my mouth dry and gaping, my knees knocking, I lost all awareness of the boy and thought only of approaching death. Standing but two yards away, the Indians observed us with deep interest, as I might watch a freak on public show at a village fair. Their tongues gabbled all at once, but in their faces was no hint of fear.

Then I heard the boy's broken voice in my ear, "Shoot them. Shoot them now."

Even if I had considered this possibility, I knew my hand was too stiff with terror to raise and fire the musket. I was appalled at my own cowardice, and stood stupidly rigid, vaguely aware of a warm flush upon my leg. I had urinated— and to my horror this had not gone unnoticed. Almost at once the voices fell, and the tip of a spear crossed the space between us to touch, very gently, the spreading stain upon my trousers. Gasping, I flattened myself farther against the sled, and momentarily the spear was withdrawn to the accompaniment of nervous laughter from my tormentors.

At this, the boy could take no more. Pushing forward from behind my shoulder where he had been cowering, he cried out, "Kill us! Go on, kill us!" Then he fell to his knees before them, as if begging for the thrust that would send him to his Maker.

There followed a brief silence, then a rush of laughter,

and in a few seconds the group broke up, some going one way to the sandhills, some another, to inspect the sled. In this brief interval, I managed to move away, allowing the Indians to freely circle our goods, jabbing and testing with their spears. They touched nothing with their bare hands. Then, from behind the sled where I could not see, came an awful cry. I thought at first that one of the Indians had injured another, then further cries followed and, leaving the boy, I moved a little to one side to see. Here were the two old men gesturing with great excitement toward the grass tree pole that the boy had wedged in our load. From its topmost point our foolish banner of happier days, the white stocking, had caught the sea breeze and now swelled out full of wind. It was the appearance of this white and ghostly limb, apparently living but attached to no body, that had caused the commotion.

Seeing that it was the Indians' turn to be overcome with fear, I leaped upon the load and with a series of swift movements pulled down the pole and removed the stocking. From my vantage point on the sled I now held out this limp and formless object, offering it as a sign of peace. But while their noises ceased, the fear would not leave their faces, nor would they advance so much as a footstep to further inspect the cause of their dismay. Instead, they exchanged swift glances and, within moments, had trotted away up the beach, leaving us bewildered and alone.

Hardly had we taken the chance to accuse each other of cowardice, than upon the sandhills they appeared again, this time numbering well above fifty, among them women and children. I said to the boy, "We must meet them. To stay here is foolishness," and not waiting for his approval, I walked unarmed toward the entire tribe, for that was what I concluded was now staring down upon me.

As I reached the base of the sandhills, several of the males came forward. There was no fear in their faces and I tried to present the same attitude, extending my hand in greeting and welcoming them in my own tongue—foolish as that may seem.

When at last we came close enough to shake hands, this courtesy was refused, but they did lay their hands upon me, first stroking my hair and beard (which was grown as long and dark as their own), then the skin of my face and arms. I did not resist, although I was still trembling with fear, and presently many bodies were about me, men and women, calling out and laughing and touching.

My clothes seemed to attract the greatest interest, and these I allowed them to feel until, growing braver, I bent forward and pulled my shirt over my head, holding it out for them to touch.

Of course, this was a stupid action, being no different in kind from holding out the limp stocking, and they screamed in terror in precisely the same way as they had done earlier on the beach. I now began to understand the cause of their fear: in removing my shirt I had quite miraculously skinned myself, without losing so much as a drop of blood or uttering a whimper of pain.

I dropped the shirt to the ground at once, and proceeded to show them by signs with my hands that the structure of my chest was the same as theirs, and my back likewise, turning it to them in a show of courage that amazed even myself.

Having made this clear, there remained the problem of my trousers. These I was truly afraid to remove but my audience was not so easily satisfied. Although there appeared to be smiles and friendship on all faces, I could not help but feel the touches of the hands grow heavier and the prodding of the spears more insistent. At last, with the conviction that it was shame rather than fear that had led me to be so stubborn, I released the fastening of my belt and eased the trousers from my body. In so doing I stood before the Indians completely naked, and a silence that I found unbearable fell upon the tribe. Presently I began to speak, and although I knew they could understand none of what I said, still I talked on, telling anything and everything about the journey and what I had to offer for trade. Not a word was spoken in response until, just as I was about to call on the boy for help, I felt the touch of a hand on my buttocks, and another on my back, my thighs, and I was touched again all over, while the voices were once more raised in a great babbling.

Then I turned to find the boy. Stumbling and crawling, he had been driven up the beach and now, following the completion of my inspection, I supposed he was about to undergo the same.

Again I was wrong. Although at first the tribe touched him as they had me, there were marked differences in their response. They would not touch his hair, which had been bleached white in the sun and now hung long and straight to his shoulders, nor could they comprehend his eyes, which unlike mine or theirs, were the palest blue—and the men withdrew from him, leaving only the women to ogle and poke.

I said, "Be calm. They will not hurt you." But this was not in the boy's nature and he twisted to face everybody who touched him, so that he began to spin wildly and to appear foolish.

I grew afraid and cried out to him. "Don't! Take off your clothes and it will be over." He would not listen and instead screamed obscenities at them, finally tossing himself in a heap on the ground.

The women fell upon him at once, and instead of allowing him to undress with dignity, tore the clothes from him and tossed them to their fellows who threw them about further. The mystery of removing the skin seemed forgotten.

Then a shout went up and the women fell back, covering their mouths and eyes. The men came forward, listened, and moved toward the naked boy writhing on the sand before them. There was much pointing and exclamation, then a spear thrust forward and the boy lay still in terror. I thought surely he had brought about his own death, but this was not so. Ever so gently, the spear touched his privates, carefully examining his manhood. The women drew closer, looking first at his nakedness, then at my own.

The purpose of these actions was a mystery to me, until I resorted to reason. His hair was fair, fine and long, mine shorter, coarse and dark; his eyes were pale as water, mine black as their own. In our bodies there was no comparison, for though he stood taller than me, I was clearly the more powerful of build, our weeks of starvation notwithstanding. In observing these physical signs, the Indians had taken the boy to be a female, even my mate.

This conclusion was apparent to me but of no worth to the boy, who proceeded to whimper and snivel in the most dreadful manner. When the Indians had done with their prodding, I moved to help him, but as I did so I saw there was something else that had taken their eye, and now caught my own.

Around the boy's neck hung a cord of leather, and threaded upon it was a golden ring, its single red stone gleaming in the sun.

This concludes the second installment of the Loos journal.

Item 19

Advertisement from the Standard
Wednesday, July 30, 1986

Missing Relic
A Public Appeal

In recent weeks members of the public have been well informed regarding investigations into certain historic relics, including an iron pot, a journal, and a human hand, found in Cliff Cave 327, Lower Murchison District, in April 1986.

It is a source of concern to the Institute of Maritime Archaeology conducting these investigations that another object, namely:

A GOLD RING

believed to be upon the human hand at the time of its discovery, has not been recovered for analysis.

If any member of the public has information regarding the whereabouts of this object, they are asked to contact the Institute by phoning (008) 232 7520. (This is a toll-free number.)

Dr. Hope Michaels, Director
Institute of Maritime Archaeology
Perth, Western Australia

Item 20

Messenger, Midway Roadhouse

About this time I was having some personal problems and it was necessary to take a few days off.

I traded with Kratz for a chain bolt (I didn't tell him what it was for) and fitted it to my bedroom door. I felt I needed that security. I think it is important to stand back and look at yourself sometimes and say, "Enough is enough. Take it easy." Also my chest had been playing up. I was feverish and wheezing.

I spent a lot of time in my room working on a new project, using the fine wire Kratz had given me. The idea for this came from a comic called *Alien Invaders* that turned up with some magazines. The comic itself was very childish, about creatures from Planet Death that invaded the earth, but there was one difference: these creatures had the appearance of humans. They watched a ball game, walked down a city street, and rubbed shoulders with office workers in an elevator, all unnoticed. Not until the last moment had they been spotted (just when they were about to take over the world) and only because some nosy kid caught sight of their masks, and lifted a flap of rubbery skin to expose their otherness, kept secret underneath. Then they were destroyed.

The part that interested me was when the kid pulled the camouflage skin off. The illustrator drew this very well, each frame of the comic showing a little more of the pale and formless flesh until finally I could see the entire skeleton beneath—the alien substructure. I enjoyed seeing the different stages of this process, the sequencing of it all, and the bones themselves were very beautiful, detailed and precise. This comic, and the fact that I had the wire, gave me the idea for the project. I thought of calling it the "Skeleton Maker," but later settled for the "Life Frame," which sounded more scientific and mature. I was interested in seeing a complete skeleton and the process involved in creating one. Basically, I would use the wire to weave a frame or net to encase a creature (probably one of the lizards that squatted in the sun on the cliffs) and put this on a meat-ant nest. These ants have a burning bite and their vicious pincers could strip the flesh off a carcass in a few hours.

I could have picked up a flattened lizard off the highway, but for obvious reasons that would not give the same result.

I also took my time experimenting with the wire (it was flat black—I usually preferred the bright metals), manipulating it with my fingers and knotting it with pliers, until I understood its special qualities. I was just as careful to study the net design I would use when weaving. An environmental magazine had an article on bird smuggling and featured excellent photographs of the wire-netting tubes the birds were transported in. I decided to use one of those as my model.

When my mother called the doctor to come to check out my chest, I made sure these things were put away—and the ring too, of course.

With all my problems, the ring was not neglected. It was scrubbed daily with a toothbrush dipped in alcohol, then polished with a soft cloth. Against the light from my window it would glow like a living thing. The stone was so wonderfully clean that I could see myself reflected in it, looking back as if to say, "What are you doing out there?" But the truth was, while it looked fantastic, nothing actually happened and, every night, instead of getting out, like before, I was left with fever and terrible dreams and my mother bashing at the door.

I can't be sure about certain things (even now it's too soon to know) but I think this failure to perform had something to do with ownership, my confusion about the identity of the ring owner. As I said, I can't be sure. Or it could have been the publicity, the advertisement in the paper. Now the ring was everybody's business, everybody's property. Maybe it was that loss of privacy and also knowing someone had been at my place on the headland, possibly following me.

I worked with the wire on the Life Frame to stop thinking like that, or I could sometimes tune out by watching the garage, or the Roadhouse, or even the motel sign flashing.

Quite often I would see the other Steven Messenger, cooler than ever, waiting under the sign, pacing backward and forward. He wore a red T-shirt and white straight-legged jeans. They were so snug his body moved inside them like a second skin. He had tooled leather boots with silver toe-capping, the heels caked with red mud, or maybe blood. Over his shoulder was a bedroll and at the base of the sign was an overnight bag.

I could see him pacing at any time. I didn't need the ring for that. But I couldn't fly, or get back to that amazing girl, Ela. Those days were over.

So I concentrated on the weaving. I had been thinking about the design of a base for the Life Frame. The wire frame itself was like a cylindrical cage that would encase the creature for the experiment, and I needed to carefully consider the type of base this frame would attach to, and how it would be placed—either on or between the ant mounds. The best mounds were near the headland, just behind my special place. I knew I would have to take the frame up there to check the design.

But there was the business of the hand scratched on the rock. I had not been up to the headland since the day I saw that hand. I wanted to go and see it again, to check if I was mistaken. I thought maybe it was just my imagination, and now I needed to see if it was gone—or had ever been there. Since I was not feeling 100 percent myself, I waited for a fine warm day and one when my mother had a double shift. That gave me the chance to take my time. I put the Life Frame in a backpack, and wore the ring under my shirt. (I was still not game to wear it out in the open, even along the cliffs.) Then I left.

I was in no hurry—I even stopped once or twice to chuck rocks at the gulls—so in no way was I ready for what happened. Nothing could have prepared me for it. Except I think I could have used the ring, but I only thought of that later.

As I came closer to the headland, I was considering turning a bit to the right, more away from the cliff edge and into the low bushes, to have a look at the ant mounds. There were maybe twelve or fifteen there, in a sort of colony, each mound about eight inches high and two feet in diameter. You could just barely walk between them. If you walked on one, the ants would pour out, and they were vicious. So I was about to go in that direction when the feeling of being watched started up, the same as it had the night of the letter, when I was walking back to the Roadhouse.

I looked over my shoulder, half expecting to see Kratz, although I knew that he was at school, way down the highway.

With about a hundred yards to go, the feeling grew so strong I stopped completely and turned. There was nothing, but all the same I veered quite sharply away from the edge, heading inland where the bushes were thicker and higher and I could double back. I was thinking, "Whoever you are, at least I'm going to see you first."

Moving in an arc, I came onto the path about fifty yards below where I had begun. This time I kept the path beside me, about two yards to my left, just to be sure. I made it almost all the way to the tip of the headland without drawing breath, and by the time I got there my chest was aching.

I stopped for a last look in the low bushes at the point where I step down into the rock, when I felt something brush against my leg. I jumped back, but what came next made me feel sick.

Looking up at me from the hole in the rock was the Abo who came out to school, Charlie Sunrise. Before I could do anything his hand shot out and got a grip around my ankle.

From then on, everything happened so fast. I pulled back and kicked to shake him off but he was coming up out of the hole and the more I pulled the more I helped him out.

He was saying, "Come here. Come here," but I wasn't going to be murdered by any Abo.

Just as he was coming up over the edge, I kicked forward so he lost his grip and my foot got him on the side of his head, at the temple. He fell backward and for a second we stared at each other, trying to work out what was going on. Blood started coming from his head. He must have felt it and wiped it away with the back of his hand. I saw the twisted fingers. His eyes looked more bloodshot than I could remember.

All I wanted was to get out of there but I had backed myself into the bushes and between me and him I saw the ants. When I was kicking I must have stood on a mound. These were the red meat-ants. They were pouring out everywhere, like the ground was moving in a thick red mass, but he kept crawling up out of the hole and his hands were covered in them, right up his arms, even under his sleeves.

I told him to leave me alone and that I had friends

nearby and he should get lost. I was leaning back farther and farther into the bushes while he was still crawling. When I ran out of threats, he stood up facing me, and started talking and pointing behind him.

I couldn't understand a word he was saying, but from the signs he made with his hand I guessed he was talking about something falling over the edge of the cliff. I thought maybe he had dropped his wine over the side. Everyone said the mission blacks were winos. I was watching his face and his hand but I could see the ants too. They were all over his feet. Hundreds of them, with their biting pincers. He took no notice. Then he said plainly, "That writing," and I saw he wasn't pointing over the cliff edge at all, but into the hole in the rock, and the writing he was talking about was the word I scratched, ELA. That's what was on his mind. The girl's name.

He said, "Did you write that? Did you write the name on the rock?"

I didn't say anything but took the chance to get myself up out of the bushes.

"I seen you here," he said. "You been here many times. Six or eight times I seen you here. Even at night I seen you up here."

Then I am sure he said, "The last time I seen your light . . ." I have thought about that since, and I am sure he said just those words, but he was raving on and on about the name and how I scratched it, and I can't be certain.

He said, "You come up here and you scratched that name . . . with what? This?" He grabbed at my belt buckle and I jumped back.

His curled up hands were opening and closing and the blood was running down the side of his face. I could see ants on his chest.

I should have said, "Shut your mouth—shut your mouth or I'll wire it shut." I was bigger than him. I could have whipped the Frame out of the backpack and crushed the wire into his face.

The other Steven Messenger would have done that. But this Abo was grinning at me, like I was a joke. He looked right into me, the same as he did at school, straight into my insides, under my clothes.

He said, "I know you and where you live. I seen you in your house. On your nice clean bed."

Then he bent down and, with one finger, drew a shape in the sand of the ant mound. I could have run but I didn't. I was watching the ants go mad and when he finished I saw what he had done (until the ants covered it). Five straight lines and an upturned triangle. A hand. The same as the one on the rock. I knew right away that he was the one who had followed me that night.

He said, "You seen and heard enough for one day. But I know more. Yes. A lot more about you. When you're ready, you come down the mission to see Charlie. If you got the guts. I'll be there. Now piss off."

He backed up toward the cliff and I went. I jumped over the mounds and ran straight down the cliff path. I ran almost all the way back to the Roadhouse, until I was behind the motel fence, then I couldn't go on and fell down on my hands and knees. My chest was terrible. I brought up phlegm and blood. I'd never been as sick as that before.

But when I had finished vomiting, the weird thing was that the ring felt warm—the first time in over a week.

Item 21

From the Standard Weekend Edition,
Saturday/Sunday, August 2/3, 1986

A Murderer's Diary
The third installment of
the journal of Wouter Loos

*This installment is translated by Professor Hans Freudenberg
and introduced by Colin Paterson, Senior Lecturer, School of
Comparative Anthropology, Brisbane.*

The second installment of Wouter Loos's journal, which appeared in the *Standard* a week ago, has raised further issues in one of the most controversial topics under consideration by anthropologists today: the history and practice of cannibalism.

In his journal, Loos tells how both he and fellow castaway, Jan Pelgrom, feared that they might be eaten by other humans—although initially these fears arose for quite different reasons: Loos was terrified that he might be killed and eaten by his companion, Pelgrom; while Pelgrom ironically considered himself to be under precisely the same threat from the "Indians."

Although readers who have followed the castaways' fortunes will appreciate the poetic justice of seeing Pelgrom suffer, there is every reason to pause and reflect upon which episode would have been the most likely to take place: white eating white, or black eating white.

If historical precedent and current research are applied,

there can be only one answer: not a single documented, eye-witness account exists of an Australian Aborigine (Loos's Indian) having killed and eaten a white person. However, cases of white men eating members of their own race abound—and in these instances both personal confession and physical evidence (bodily remains) have been gathered and documented.

The doubting reader may be well advised to investigate the cases of certain European cannibals of Australia's convict days, for example, Jeffries, known also as "the monster," born at Bristol and hanged in Launceston, Tasmania, in 1826 for killing and eating a fellow convict escapee; or Alexander Pearce, hanged July 19, 1824, for escaping from custody twice, and on both occasions surviving by eating his companions. There were numerous other white cannibals in that era: Edward Broughton, Matthew Maccavoy, Richard Hutchinson, and the depraved eighteen-year-old, Patrick Fagan.

It is unfortunate, however, that old myths die hard, and the myth of cannibalism among the so-called colored races is no exception. While most myths are believed to originate from an element of fact, that "fact" may be little more than a fear—a fear that has no basis in physical reality. For example, one of the original cannibal concepts arises from the Greek myth of the Cyclops, who was not only supposed to have one eye in the middle of the forehead but also to live upon human flesh. It is interesting to note that while no intelligent twentieth-century person would accept the one-eyed element of the Cyclops myth, many might still be tempted to believe in the equally mythical feasting on human flesh.

The impact Christopher Columbus had on the development of modern attitudes toward the cannibal myth is also worth noting and correcting.

On November 23, 1492, Columbus recorded in his journal that upon nearing an island the Indians aboard called Bohio, he was told by some of them that the inhabitants were one-eyed and by others that they were cannibals, who were warlike and ate people.

This is the first recorded use of the word *cannibale,* meaning "eater of human flesh" or "cannibal" in English.

Sadly, the faults in Columbus's record, which cast serious doubts upon the value of his journal as evidence, are rarely discussed and, for too long, the western world has been fed his warped interpretation of so-called history, observed and recorded from his biased point of view. However, the long-range effect of ideas put forward by persons such as Columbus can be seen when we return to the two castaways, Loos and Pelgrom.

Although written over one hundred and thirty years after the discovery of the "New World," and on another continent, the Loos journal nevertheless shows the influence of Europe and of those who followed Columbus to conquer and sack the Americas.

Loos's language includes terms such as *cannibals, tribes of Indians, the Brazils,* and in an installment of the journal yet to be published, he refers to the fabled and long sought after land of *El Dorado*—the land of the "Man of Gold."

It therefore cannot be accepted that either Loos or Pelgrom first saw the Australian continent with a totally naive or even innocent view—in fact they brought with them a way of seeing the landscape and its inhabitants that had been heavily influenced by tales of explorers or conquistadors and the hearsay of buccaneers and fellow sailors.

The cannibal myth is just one example of this prejudicial view; and curiously enough, not a great deal has changed over the centuries. What name did young Steven Messenger give the iron pot that contained Loos's journal? Why, the "cannibal pot," of course. For whatever reason, this fear lives on.

Undated journal entries (continuing the entries for the period December 2, 1629, to December 4, 1629)

To my great relief, the Indians appeared to tire of inspecting our bodies very quickly, and drew back from us toward our sled.

It seemed that, despite our fears, we were not to be eaten, at least at this time. Perhaps the Indians considered us too thin to be worthwhile. But I was not about to spend my time pondering these matters. Collecting my scattered clothes, I dressed quickly and hurried to the beach. The boy I ignored, leaving him naked and weeping upon the sand, his stream of tears mingling with the vile mucus that flowed constantly from his nostrils. He had made no effort to clothe himself, rather he sat foolishly attempting to cover his private parts with one hand and the ring that hung about his neck with the other.

I do not believe myself to be a man of great intellect, yet I could readily conclude that, unless the stores were seen to, we should have no means of trading with these Indians and would once again face death from hunger and thirst.

There was, however, no need for concern. The Indians seemed more taken with the tracks of the sled than with the sled itself. Indeed, many of them lay with their stomachs upon the sand, examining the tracks in great detail.

Taking advantage of this calm, I buried beneath the sand the grass tree pole and its stocking banner that had caused so much concern to our earlier visitors, then set about removing the sailcloth cover from the sled that I might better display our goods for trade. I hoped above all things to gain food and water for our immediate survival and, if possible, to acquire a boat that might take us from this place when all other trading had been done.

These things were not to be. Hardly had I removed the cover and gained access to the musket and ax than a great noise went up from the tribe and I was surrounded by pressing bodies and inquiring hands. It was evident that unless I acted quickly and with great resolution these people would pilfer all my stores before trading could begin. Without hesitation I leaped upon the sled and cried out for them to stop, but this had no effect and indeed some of the little ones, overcome with excitement and possessed of no fear, climbed up beside me and were jumping upon the goods with great delight.

Above the general uproar I heard the boy's voice calling, "Shoot them, Wouter! Shoot!"

I turned to see him running from the sandhills, still in the process of pulling on his trousers. Considering the circumstances, his advice was quite sound, although I would not shoot into the crowd. Rather, I raised the musket above my head and fired one ball—and the effect of the sound was immediate. First there fell a wondrous calm, then a commotion such as I have never heard, and in a few moments the beach was deserted.

I looked down at the boy, who stood beside the sled. "They are gone," I said, "and may not return," but hardly had I spoken when, above the sandhills, they appeared again.

This time there were only men, and as they advanced it was quite clear that the mood of the encounter had changed.

"Quickly," the boy said. "Fire again. Kill one and be done with it."

This was an action I could not take—more out of common sense that any notion of nobility. If I had killed one of their number, then all chance of trade would be lost, and any possible means of escape. Further, with but one musket, which was slow to load, and an ax, there was little hope of fending off the dozen or so warriors who now advanced upon us.

There appeared but one hope for survival. Dropping to the sand I groped about for the stocking banner I had so recently buried and, finding it, commenced waving the ridiculous object to and fro in the air, causing the stocking to fly out, full of wind, as it had before. While this did not produce the same effect—no doubt some of the number before me had seen it that morning—it did nevertheless cause the advance to halt for a parley, thus providing the time I needed.

In an instant I had opened one of the small chests, and having grasped the first items of trade I happened upon—these being the strands of glass beads—I tossed them with all my might into the air where they circled, glinting and shining to great effect, finally falling upon the beach at the feet of our would-be attackers.

At this there arose a cry of fear, but then as the colorful appearance of the beads became evident, and the fact that they could do no harm quite obvious, first one, then another of the warriors advanced to pick them up. Having done so, each withdrew a short distance to examine his find, or consulted with another in an excited tone.

I waited, and in no time the Indians turned again to me, evidently hoping for more. I quickly obliged, offering this time a handful of black iron nails, which fell to the sand with a tinkling sound. This offering was received with a mixture of confusion and delight.

It was clear to me that having first received the beads,

the Indians were expecting more ornamentation—and here the nails had them confounded. But when one warrior experienced the sharpness of a nail point and another tested the hardness of the metal in his teeth, the value of this item was beyond compare, and before I could think of what to offer next—if indeed I were to offer any more at all without some return—they were clamoring upon me once again.

Nor were these warriors long alone; their joyous whooping and calling attracted the remainder of the tribe, who clearly had withdrawn no great distance beyond the sandhills, and presently the boy and I found ourselves forced away from the sled by their crowding bodies, having no hope of intervening, while our goods were taken from us with complete abandon.

I confess to my shame that upon witnessing this loss of all my hopes, either to do well for the Company or escape this frightful place, I fell to my knees weeping—and the boy, ever ready to express defeat, likewise joined me in this foolish activity.

Presently, however, the tribe seemed to lose interest in the contents of the sled and wandered off beyond the sandhills, some carrying many things, others none.

When we were left quite alone, the boy and I set about recovering what remained. Scattered upon the sand were many of the white stockings. These I had removed from the iron pot to make room for more valuable goods the day before setting out but, apart from the musket and ax that we had kept with us, there was very little else; only the sled itself (the rope harness had gone) and miraculously, the iron pot, which perched upon the sled's bare wooden platform.

Perhaps it was the pot's weight that caused the Indians to leave it, or their inability to unfasten the timber and metal clamps that secured its lid. I will never know, but the fact that it remained untouched filled me with some hope, for in it were secured the following goods:

1 set of flints with tinder box
1 burning glass
2 green apothecary jars of ointment
1 roll of thread and needles
wooden toys from Nüremberg
a number of white stockings as packing
this journal and writing material

To some, this may seem little cause for rejoicing, but I was glad at least that even if I should fail in all else, I might yet leave a record of my attempts to do well. In this regard, I admit, that having undone the clamps securing the lid of the pot, I clasped the journal to my breast.

Unfortunately my joy was to be short-lived, for the boy now demanded to know our future prospects, and I could offer him no reasonable answer. As we were now utterly without food or water, my vessels of muddy ooze having been stolen, to continue our walk would be folly. The day was all but over, and I doubted that we would live to see another.

The possibility of further contact with the Indians, whereby we might offer our remaining goods for victuals and shelter, also seemed foolish, as these persons merely took, offering nothing in exchange. Moreover, the boy remained in abject terror of the tribe, and expected, I believe, that I would somehow provide for his life. I therefore decided upon the only action possible, and leaving him with the sled and all its contents—including the musket and ax—I set off to follow the tribe in the hope that, having taken our all, they might offer us the little we needed to survive.

Before I set out, the boy drew me to him, embracing me, and swearing that at no time had he intended me harm. This I accepted in the spirit it was offered, and promising I would not leave him to die alone, set off across the beach.

Having followed the tracks of the Indians for a short distance beyond the sandhills, I found to my great joy that they led by a series of reedy pools, each brimming with fresh water. At the first of these I fell upon my knees to slake the thirst I had suffered so many days, then feeling more able to face whatever may come, I continued on my way.

Presently, the tracks led toward a pleasant grove of fine trees, too open to be called a forest but sufficiently timbered to provide protection for a group of neat, low huts, dome-shaped, and constructed of marvelously woven boughs. These were the homes of the Indians who had taken our goods, for not only did I recognize some of their number— the old men with gray beards being remarkable—I could also see, throughout the camp, individuals and small groups displaying or experimenting with our goods, which they had so recently acquired.

Gathering sufficient courage to enter the area, I first approached one group, then another, asking for their head man or leader. As it was obvious that my native tongue was unknown to them, I spoke English and Spanish (for I knew a little of both) but to no avail. While all seemed quite happy to mimic my voice, or laugh along with me, not one understood a word I said.

Next, thinking that perhaps the language of signs might help, with a stick I drew in the dust the shape of a crown, with a simple cross rising from the center, in order to represent the presence of a Christian ruler.

This sign provoked much discussion and I was pleased when one of the old gray-bearded men took the stick from me and drew a further representation in the earth beside mine. At first it seemed he had done no more than repeat my own system of lines, but then his message became quite clear: in the dust at my feet was drawn a sailing vessel complete with masts and yardarms—no doubt this was what the poor fellow considered my crown and cross had represented. Nor could I have been more delighted when upon finishing his work he took me by the arm and, leading me to a sandy mound beyond the camp, pointed Northward. By the last rays of the sun, I could see a distant range of rugged mountains, now bathed in the loveliest golden light, and I gathered from his excited talk and repeated gestures that here I would find a vessel such as the one he had drawn—or indeed a harbor of vessels.

Throughout this episode, the wonderful aroma of baking flesh, emanating from a central fireplace, had kept me constantly aware of my own hunger and now I grew bold enough to indicate my need for food—which was done by placing my fingers in my mouth. Thankfully, this sign was recognized and I was immediately offered a portion of white flesh from whatever animal they were roasting in their ashes. This I devoured heartily, burning my mouth in the process.

Finding myself so well received, I decided to return at once for the boy, who no doubt believed from my long absence that I had been killed. With a light heart I hurried back to the beach but, to my annoyance, I found the sled unattended and no sign of him anywhere. After calling several times, with no response, my anger turned to fear that he may have been kidnapped by the Indians and I was about to return to them when suddenly he hailed me from the sandhills.

I turned to answer but was struck dumb by the sight he presented. It was now quite dark, yet from his head radiated a soft light, the like of which I have never seen, except perhaps in images of the Saints. As he approached I stood with my back against the sled, waiting, but with each step the glow seemed to fade, and when he had reached me not a sign of his earlier glory remained. There is no doubt that I looked as if I had seen a spirit, and I told him so. At once his hand went to his chest, uncovered since he had been so crudely undressed, and touched the ring that hung there. Then he laughed, explaining all away as the last rays of the setting sun falling upon his pale hair, and demanding that I tell him the more important issues of my contact with the Indians.

This I was happy to do, and with my sworn assurance that he would come to no harm, he followed me, first to the ponds where he drank his fill, then, with every evidence of rising fear, on to the Indians' camp. By the time we arrived night had fallen and while the central fire still glowed fiercely, I could see no sign of our hosts anywhere about. This curious circumstance led me to believe that the camp had been no more than a daytime base, but then, as I moved closer to the fire and hopefully a meal, I realized my error. Scattered about underfoot, in various shallow depressions in the warm sand, were my earlier companions, their dark skins disguising their sleeping forms among the deepening shadows of the night. Therefore, as our presence seemed to pose no threat whatsoever, for indeed there was not so much as a guard to be seen, we foraged about the fireplace for the remains of the evening meal. Little enough was to be found once we had cleared away the many dogs that hung about, but as the boy had eaten nothing since killing our own unfortunate animal, I saw he was not particular in the choice of scraps he crammed into his eager mouth.

When he had eaten, I persuaded him to help me retrieve the sled from the beach, placing it temporarily under cover of dense bushes near the ponds. Then, being near exhaustion, we returned within sight of the camp fire and, having selected a spot at some distance from the nearest Indian, lay down in the sand and slept.

And so it was that we were accepted by these people and allowed to remain among them. Here also we have regained some of our strength, being well provided with food, and having taken for ourselves a hut that was not in use. I am hopeful that this protection, however rugged, may also bring an end to the boy's fever and fluxes. He breathes like a man who has not long to live.

Each day I have been able to write in this journal, though I fear that my ink will not last and I may be forced to discover some means of producing more, or abandon my record altogether.

This concludes the third installment of the Loos journal.

Item 22

Photocopied from Early Australian Shipwrecks *by*
Charles W. Smith
(Ashley Publications, Melbourne, 1973, pp. 3–4)

... There is an increasing amount of information—much of it pure speculation—that the so-called Mahogany Ship, said to be buried in sandhills near Warrnambool, Victoria, was the first European vessel wrecked upon the Australian coast.

Anthropologist Aldo Massola has on record a traditional tale from the Yangeri tribe (who inhabited the Warrnambool area) that "yellow men" were said to have appeared well before the coming of the Europeans and that these yellow men had intermarried with the tribe. It has been claimed that Nellie Cain, one of the last Yangeris:

> was quite different from an ordinary Aboriginal. Her color, her hair, the general contour of her countenance, and particularly her profile, all were said to suggest some foreign strain.[1]

Historian K. G. McIntyre goes into great detail to establish that the Mahogany Ship wreck was a Portugese caravel, part of a small fleet led by the navigator Cristovão De Mendonça, which was driven ashore by gales in about 1522, just thirty years after Columbus stumbled upon the Americas.[2]

The fact that the timbers of the Mahogany Ship have never been analyzed by modern scientists (the wreck was last sighted in 1880) has not helped prove McIntyre's case.

There can be no doubt, however, that the first authenticated European shipwreck upon the Australian coast was that of the British East Indiaman *Trial*, or *Tryal*, which went down on rocks north of Barrow Island, Western Australia, shortly after 11 PM on May 25, 1622.

The *Trial* had been on her maiden voyage from Plymouth bound for Java via the Cape of Good Hope. Her English captain, John Brookes, decided to risk taking the newly discovered direct route—straight across the Indian Ocean, then north upon sighting the mysterious Southland—but he had no experienced navigator. As a result, the vessel struck uncharted rocks some forty miles from the mainland, holing her badly. No sooner had the seriousness of the situation been ascertained than Captain Brookes gathered the most valuable elements of the cargo, the chests of gold, then abandoned

---

1. *Journey to Aboriginal Victoria*, Rigby, Adelaide, 1969, p. 38.
2. *The Secret Discovery of Australia*, Souvenir Press, Sydney, 1977.

ship with seven others in a small skiff. Within an hour the first mate, Thomas Bright, did likewise, taking thirty-six more people in a longboat. Both Captain Brookes's and Bright's vessels arrived safely in Java by early July.

The remainder of the passengers and crew aboard the *Trial* were left to go down with the ship, on a clear night with a calm sea.

Current research indicates that Captain Brookes and some of his crew may have landed upon the Australian mainland in the area of Point Cloates on May 2, 1622—that is, three weeks before the *Trial* was wrecked a further 125 miles to the north.

It is quite possible that Aboriginal representations of a European sailing vessel—clearly showing its hull, decking, masts, and sails—which appear in rock galleries in the Cape Range National Park only thirty miles north of Point Cloates, were painted some three hundred years ago to commemorate the *Trial*'s visit to these shores.

Of course, in areas where such landings or shipwrecks occurred, there are always references to mysterious white-skinned visitants in local Aboriginal folklore. One of the most persistent of these myths is told by the people of the lower Ashburton River, about sixty-two miles south of where the *Trial* was wrecked. They say that, long ago but not in the dream time, there appeared from among the sandhills a red and white child—a female—with hair like the sun. None of the local women could claim her as a child returned from the spirit world and, since she had no knowledge of tribal language, the child was taken south, along the coastal trading routes, until she reached the Murchison River. Here, the people living in the area of the Wilgamia red ochre deposits claimed her at once, recognizing her as one of their own long lost children by the curious red coloration of her skin.

So much for myths. What we can be certain of is that the wreck of the *Trial* was discovered by divers in 1969.[3]

Item 23

Messenger, Midway Roadhouse

After I got away from Charlie Sunrise on the headland and made it back to our trailer, I undressed and stood under the shower. My mother was at work and I used as much water as I wanted. I stood there until I could feel my breathing start to slow down. I locked myself in my room then and lay down on the bed.

I remember watching the motel sign for a while, trying to stop myself thinking.

Next thing, Charlie's face was at the window. I tried to get up, but I couldn't. I was lying on the bed, naked, and his bloodshot eyes were staring at me. Then the window started sliding open, very slowly, leaving a space right over my stomach, and his black hand came through, glossy like a snake's head. I flattened myself, pulling my stomach in, but the ring was there, coiled in its leather strip directly beneath the hand. I could do nothing. Then the snake hand was followed by a snake arm and I heard a hissing laugh from the grinning

3. While Smith discounts the case of the red and white girl as myth, it may not be. The red ochre deposits at Wilgamia (*Wilgie* meaning red ochre, *mia* meaning place in local Aboriginal dialect) have been famous along the Aboriginal trade routes of the Western Australian coast for centuries. After her visit to the Wilgamia deposits in 1911, Daisy Bates records: "I came out a woman in red. There was not an inch of me that had not been ochred all over . . . smeared with the greasy stuff." (*The Passing of the Aborigines*, Panther, London, 1972, p. 132.) Other cases of castaway white children, documented by Jill Boxtel in *From Other Worlds* (1985), are referred to in Item 25 of these documents—Ed.

mouth, and the fingers were sliding over my stomach, to touch the ring. I sat up then, because I was going to be sick.

The window was shut. There was no face. No hand. The ring was still around my neck. The motel sign blinked in daylight. Everything had gone crazy. Nothing was right anymore.

I pulled the ring off and chucked it against the wall— but it bounced right back. I thought, "Okay, I can fix that," and stuck it in my dresser drawer, figuring it could straighten itself out there.

After that I felt better. I dressed and tried to be normal again. I did a pile of homework and cleaned up the kitchen for my mother. When the bus came in I went over to see Kratz at the garage. The Dream Machine was almost ready for the road, he said.

I watched him for a while then went back under the wire and started to get supper. My mother came in after her shift finished at 6 o'clock and we ate together. She said I looked better. I read the papers and went to bed.

I didn't slide the lock on my door—I said to myself that was crazy. But it wasn't so crazy. Not at all. Because what happened that night was fantastic.

I put my hands behind my head and looked out into the darkness. Always the same: the lights of the Roadhouse, the occasional roar of a rig and its thousand lights, the motel sign. Much later, in the small hours, about two or three, the Roadhouse lights go down. Just a little, but enough to accept the night, or maybe the morning coming.

This night, after I was so sick, I saw the lights dip and I knew I had to sleep. I pulled the sheet up and turned on my pillow with my back to the window. I closed my eyes. As I did, I saw a glow from the dresser from inside the drawer.

I counted like I do, ten, twenty, thirty, forty, and at a hundred I looked. There wasn't any doubt. From the drawer where I had put the ring, right at the very back, came a yellow light.

I knew then that everything was okay. I wasn't crazy. The ring was mine for sure. I would never give it back.

First thing next morning (that was a Saturday), I paid Kratz another visit. He already had his head under the hood of his machine. He was fiddling with wires and swearing. I stood back a bit and watched. His short, thick fingers were filthy, his fingernails were split and filled with grease, like black crescent moons.

I thought of the black hands of the Abo, Charlie, and how I had scrubbed my leg where he grabbed me.

There was sweat running down from Kratz's hair, along his cheek. I saw a little drop run along his jaw. That's when I spotted this line of dark hair—very fine, each hair curved parallel to the next, right where the jaw became the neck. I couldn't help staring. I wondered if under that was a seam, or a flap of skin I could lift and tear off, the same as in that comic, *Alien Invaders,* then all of a sudden he turned.

He had a big grin. I could see his white teeth, perfectly even.

"Knew you were there, Stevo," he said. "I can always tell when it's you."

I thought this was a lie, but it was important to play up to Kratz because of his moods, so I just laughed and asked him why he was swearing. He said it was the headlights. There was a short in the wiring that he couldn't find. I might have been interested in this, its being wiring, and all, but it was so filthy and greasy under the hood that I let it pass and nodded.

Then Kratz said, "You must be a lot better, up and about so early," and I said, "Yes."

He gave me a look as if he expected me to say more, but

I didn't. Instead I walked around the vehicle as if I was interested. Which I was—in a way.

I think I already mentioned that it was a Ford pickup. Because of years of exposure to salt wind, the body panels had been eaten out with rust and the entire vehicle seemed to be camouflaged, with splotches in green and brown and different shades of gray.

There were jagged pieces of metal protruding from fenders and door panels. There were no turn signals and no grille—the radiator had red and orange rust streaks running from top to bottom. The truck bed was made of splintered gray planks that had been bolted to two wooden cross pieces attached to the chassis with metal brackets. I bent down and looked under. There was no exhaust pipe, but the muffler was there, wired on. The back tires were so bald and shiny I could nearly see my face in them.

"Is this safe?" I said.

Kratz thought for a moment. "Maybe not," he said. "But it runs."

He opened the driver's door and got in. I noticed there was no floor covering and there were rust holes around the brake and clutch. He didn't shut the door but gave the accelerator a few pumps and turned on the ignition. The engine gave a cough and a backfire like a gunshot, then I could hear this deep chugging.

"See," he said. "Goes like a beauty."

It was true. Although there were rattles and shakes, I could tell it would make it down the highway.

I went around to the passenger's door and was struggling with the handle when Kratz laughed.

"Sorry. No go on that one. You have to get in the window." So I looked in.

Half of the seat was gone. It was just a pile of old stuffing and wire springs.

"Bush rats," Kratz said, and started laughing again. "A whole family of them in there until I took over. Don't worry. They've gone now."

There was no windshield either. Just a hole.

I said, "Kratz, you couldn't drive this. The wind would blow you away."

But he shook his head. "I've got a new windshield on order."

Then he reached under the seat and pulled out a pair of welding goggles with smoky plastic lenses.

"Borrowed these to use until the real thing arrives."

He was looking at me so full of himself that I figured it was the right time to ask.

I said, "So when could you take me for a run?"

Right away, his face went flat. He put the goggles back under the seat and got out. I stood there, waiting, but he went around to the front and closed the hood.

Next thing he said, "Why do you have to come and ask stupid questions like that? You know I haven't got a license."

I knew he could drive all right. I had seen him take cars out for test runs with the mechanics. I didn't think it was stupid to ask. I thought he would be okay but, like I said, he was unpredictable.

"I needed to find out," I said. "It's important."

His eyes flicked when I said that, so he was interested. I told him, if he could drive me to a particular place, there were three *Playboys* in it for him, as a trade. He looked at me as if I were crazy. I said they were all recent, and complete with centerfolds. Then he came right up to me, and looked straight into my face.

"How could anyone grow so tall and still be so stupid?"
That's exactly what he said. I never forgot that.

He said, "Why would I want to get arrested for three
girly magazines? I could take a squint through the motel wall
anytime if that's what I was after."

I didn't have a comeback so I turned away, but he
grabbed my shoulder and pulled me back. (I hated that, when
he touched me.)

He said, "Listen, if this trip is so urgent, why don't you
tell your mom? She could easily get a trucker to take you."
(He meant one of the truck drivers my mother was friendly
with at the cafe. Because my father was away so often, the
truckers were always making passes at my mother.)

I shook his hand off me and told him that where I was
going had to be kept private. At least only between him and
me, and one other. Certainly not my mother.

He was softening up, I could tell by his face.

He said, "Jeez, Stevo. Come and tell me, if it's so important."

He went over by some fuel cans and sat on one that was
lying on its side. I followed him, but I wouldn't sit down.

"Well," he said, "spit it out."

That's when I took the risk and told him right out I
wanted a lift down to the Abo mission. I told him about my
place on the headland, the sign of the hand on the rock, and
meeting Charlie Sunrise. I didn't mention about the ring, or
knowing the girl's name, or the fight on the ant nests. I told
it quite differently—like old Charlie had met me down the
headland and asked for my help, that he wanted to see me
again about the mummified hand and the missing ring.

Kratz never said a word during all this. He didn't even
look at me, just kept on expanding and contracting part of a
car radio aerial he picked up off the ground.

When I finished and there was quiet, he said, "So why ask me? Why not get Sergeant Norman to go with you? He knows where the mission is as well as I do."

I said no, old Charlie only wanted us, people like him and me, because we had actually been there when the hand was discovered.

But Kratz shook his head. He said, "Just suppose I did go, and drove the machine, you realize we could get our heads bashed in? Everyone talks about what it's like down there. They live in car bodies and have dogs with rabies."

I knew what he was talking about. The mission was about half way to Hamelin, maybe twelve miles north of the Roadhouse, but off into the desert to the east. It was supposed to have been a decent place once. Some German missionaries started it up as a school and farm for what was left of the local blacks around the turn of the century. Pictures of the mission church were hanging on the walls of the Shire Council Library. I saw them whenever I was there. The church was brick and painted white. Over the door was a wooden sign that said NEULAND MISSION. But the dormitories where the Abos had to sleep looked like concentration camp huts.

Anyway, the experiment failed. No one could expect to grow anything around here. Not with this sand and no rain. Now all that anyone could see from the highway were a few rundown old buildings, some dead trees, and the gravestones in the cemetery. As far as I knew, no whites ever went to the mission now. Like Kratz said, they reckoned that behind the ruins, in among the bushes, were car bodies and shanties where blacks still lived.

That was one of the main reasons I wanted Kratz to come—to back me up. He was hard to get along with one to one because of his moods, but he was good on first appear-

ances. He seemed friendly and got people on his side—like
the time in the staff common room he gave Charlie Sunrise
his seat. He was what people call an operator.

I said, "You won't take me then?"

He pretended to ignore that, and kept fiddling with the
aerial, pushing it in and out, in and out.

So I added, "It's not for me, Kratz. It's for old Charlie.
I'd go by myself if I could drive."

He muttered something and I asked him, "What?"

Then he chucked the aerial to one side, got up, and said,
"When?"

"Tomorrow," I said. "Early."

I heard him say, "All right." Then he walked off into the
back of the garage.

When I was sure he was gone I picked up the aerial out
of the rubbish and ducked off home under the fence.

Next morning about eight o'clock, I heard Kratz calling
me and looked out the window. He was at the back of the
garage.

"All ready," he said, "if you're game."

I gave him the keep-your-voice-down sign because my
mother was home, had a shower, then went over.

Kratz was in the truck cab, lying on his back across the
seat. His head and hands were under the dash, and I could
see he was fiddling with wires again. There was heavy static
from a radio.

"Still got wiring problems," he said. "Tried to put this
radio in yesterday, but snapped off the stupid aerial. Now
when I turn on the dashlights I get the radio; turn on the
radio I get the dash . . ." He sat up then, and gave me one of
those straight-in-the-eye looks. "You know my theme song?
You know Meatloaf's *Bat Out of Hell* album? You know
'Paradise by the Dashboard Light'?"

I never had a chance to answer him. His head went back under the dash, and he started singing:

"Though it's cold and lonely in the deep dark night, I can see paradise by the dashboard light."

He twisted a couple more wires together and stood up.

"Done," he said. "Now, help me load this and we're off." He pointed to a massive metal box on the concrete beside him.

"What's that?" I said.

"Tools—essential for survival out there." He flicked his head toward the desert. "Come on, we have to tie it to the truck bed."

We left not long after that, and I asked him if he was still worried about not having a license and being picked up on the highway.

He said, "Stevo, how many police vehicles operate in this area?"

I told him "One." Everybody knew that Sergeant Norman was the only cop based at Hamelin.

"Good," he said. "And by a tremendous coincidence, that one vehicle was called out, not half an hour ago, to find a bomb planted somewhere in the high school. Get the message?"

I sat quiet then, but I did start to feel a bit sick.

It wasn't the driving, or the wind blasting my face (Kratz wore the welding goggles, but I wouldn't), it was what I had to do about facing Charlie Sunrise, and what he might tell me.

And the ring. I wore it under my shirt again, and kept thinking about it, and putting my hand up to check that it was there.

As things turned out, getting down to the mission was nothing. We were there in no time, but even though Kratz slowed down, we couldn't see any entrance or driveway. Not even a gate. We let the truck idle for a while and got out to have a look. Right at the side of the road were a few patches of scrub, maybe two to three yards high, and beyond that some headstones sticking out of long grass, then the old buildings. On the other side, in the distance, were more bushes. There was nothing else, only the highway and the red desert sand.

"What do we do now?" I said.

Kratz shrugged. "It's your party, but you're sure as hell not going to meet Charlie Sunrise out here on the highway, are you?" I didn't like him being smart right then. I said, "I mean about the pickup. It can't sit out here. You don't want to advertise."

He nodded. "I'll put it in those bushes. No one can see it there. Then you can walk."

I was ready for that. "I think you should come in too. It would look better," but Kratz was sitting there, grinning.

I said, "Look, just come in until I find Charlie. Then, if I talk to him, you can come back here."

He didn't say no, so I guessed it was okay. I got out and waited until he turned the pickup around and ran it off the shoulder of the highway into the low scrub. It was pretty well hidden. All the camouflage colors helped.

We started to walk through the long grass, and I saw the gravestones. There were some properly carved head pieces, crosses, and even an angel. I wondered if one of the German missionaries had been a sculptor. Every stone was for an Abo; I could tell by the names—a few Sunrises and Daylights, but some single names like Billy or Peter or Mary. Many stones had fallen over; some were facedown and broken. It was an awful place. Very depressing. It made me feel sicker than before.

Kratz was coming up behind me, still wearing the goggles.

I said, "You'd better take those things off your face," and he did.

After a while we came to the old buildings. I could make out which was the church even though the sign was gone, and over to one side were the remains of the big dormitories. There wasn't anything else, only red sand everywhere, and a terrible quiet.

Kratz said, "This place gives me the willies. Where are the bums everyone talks about?"

And right then the dogs started. We heard them first from way over behind the low scrub, and in a minute they came out, yellow dogs like dingoes and big blue cattle dogs too, some barking, some running around us in circles, sniffing out prints in the sand and snarling. Kratz and I were close together, nearly back to back, and we kept turning around and around on the spot while the dogs came closer, running in smaller and smaller circles.

Kratz was saying, "Oh, jeez. Oh, jeez. Oh, jeez!"

All at once a whistle came from the scrub and the dogs backed off. We waited, and a black woman came out. She was big, with a bright red dress on and no shoes.

She yelled, "You kids lost?"

But we said nothing. I think our tongues were too dry.

So she said, "Get outta here. Go on. Leave us alone," and she was turning to go.

Kratz said, "We came to see Charlie."

He said it so quickly maybe she didn't understand. She went into the bushes.

Kratz cupped his hands to his mouth and yelled, "Charlie Sunrise. Is he here?"

The woman came back then and walked right out of the scrub onto the open sand. We didn't move.

"Charlie?" she said, "You want Charlie?"

She put her hand up and waved us over. No trouble at all. I looked at Kratz and he shrugged, so over we went. About thirty feet away from her we stopped. She stood there with her hands on her hips.

"What's the matter?" she said. "What are ya standin' there for? No one's gonna eat ya."

Then she took off into the scrub and we followed, the dogs sniffing all around our legs.

Just past the bushes was a clearing with galvanized iron shacks here and there, and car bodies.

Kratz said in my ear, "This is it, buddy. Here we die!" and I could feel my chest tighten up.

There were a few old blacks around, sitting on boxes under scraps of canvas and metal that stuck out from the huts. They watched us come closer but didn't seem surprised.

The woman in the red dress went to a hut and started yelling, "Charlie, you there? Come out here, ya old bastard."

Then she went into the hut and we heard her yelling some more. Charlie came out first, bent and shading his eyes in the sun, and the woman followed him, pointing at us.

We went over to him, quite close, and when he looked up I knew he recognized me right away. He put his hands up to his eyes, as if he had light flashing in them, then he made sounds like "Uhuh, uhuh."

Kratz poked me in the side so I said, "I am Steven Messenger. I met you on the headland. This is a friend of mine. Nigel Kratzman."

Charlie made the same movement over his eyes and the same *uhuh* sound.

"I came to talk to you," I said.

My knees were knocking. I thought I'd wet myself, but I didn't.

Charlie pointed to some scrub and headed off, so I followed him.

Behind me Kratz was saying, "Die, die, soon we die," although I don't think he meant it anymore and besides, I wanted him to go.

I said, "It's okay now, Kratz. Go back to the pickup," but he wouldn't.

I said again, "It's okay. I think he only wants to talk to me. Just go back to the truck," but there was no way he was missing out. I was afraid of what he might hear.

In the scrappy shade of the scrub were car seats, some with springs sticking out like the ones in the pickup. Charlie pointed to them. We sat on the edge of one of them while he squatted in the dirt facing us, only about a yard away. All the time he was looking at me, straight at me, never at Kratz.

We sat there for a while. I looked down to break Charlie's stare and saw there were little green-blue ants crawling over my feet. (These were not meat-ants like the red ones on the headland, but I still didn't trust them.)

Then Charlie started. "You know about that ring?"

This is what I had been afraid of. He said it just like that, in front of Kratz.

I didn't open my mouth.

He said, "I know all about you. I knew you would come, when I seen you up there in the lookout."

Then Kratz said, "How do you get to the headland, Charlie? It's a long walk from here."

Charlie didn't look at Kratz, only me, but he answered him. "The sergeant takes me up. He comes in now and then. He takes me and gets me later."

I heard Kratz say under his breath, "Jeez. The sergeant comes here."

He was thinking about the truck. I wasn't. I was wondering what this Charlie knew about me and the ring.

Then he started to talk. This day he was slow and soft, so I had to lean forward. I could see flies on his face, around his eyes, and the scab on his temple where I kicked him.

"Up there, on that lookout, I see the water. I see the sky. I see the land. I say in myself, 'Where did they come from?' I say, 'Why did they come here?' But I get no answer. Nothing from the water or the sky or the land."

He stopped and brushed at the flies.

"Only the mountain rocks know all these things. The mountain rocks show me things since I was young. Yes. Maybe sixty, maybe seventy years back. Before the mission man goes from here. Well before that. When I was a young man. I walk out of here, right on the way of the desert, over where there is salt. To the bright mountain. My people's place."

He pointed his snake hand at me. "That's when I first seen you. Up there, in the bright rocks. And that ring too. I seen it all. That's a long time ago."

He said nothing then, not for a few minutes. I could feel the ants crawling up my legs. They must have been on Kratz too, but he was dead quiet, until Charlie said to him, "You drive up here? You the one who brought him here?"

Kratz nodded and Charlie said, "Sure. It's the same. All up on the rocks. I seen you there too, I seen you both, just the same."

I decided I needn't have worried too much about Kratz being there after all. This Charlie was talking such crap that no one could understand him.

Then he started again. "Not long now before I go. Not so long. I could show you the rocks . . . what they say . . . you would see—"

But Kratz cut him off. "You mean, you saw me and

Stevo in the rocks at the cliff, up at the headland? You mean those rocks? Where did you see us, Charlie?"

That was how Kratz operated. First names. Very familiar.

But the black hand was pointing off to the northeast, toward the desert. "Up there, in them bright mountains, across the salt. In my people's place. That's where you will see."

I thought the whole thing was a waste of time, and this was all rubbish. Of course Kratz leaned forward, as if he understood.

"You mean up the Nicholson Ranges? There's salt lakes up that way—and a big tribal reserve. Is that right, Charlie? Up in the Nicholson Reserve?"

Charlie was wiping his eyes, nodding.

Kratz said, "What will we see there, Charlie? Can you say?"

There was no answer.

Charlie looked at Kratz. I wanted him to drop it. To shut up. But he moved closer.

"Could you show us, Charlie? Show us the rocks? I could take you in my pickup, like the sergeant takes you to the lookout. Would that be all right?"

The old man kept nodding and I thought, "This is not possible. This can't be happening."

I felt the ring, warm against my chest, and all I wanted was to get out, to be anywhere but there.

Item 24

From the Hamelin Herald, *Monday, August 4, 1986*

Hamelin High Bomb Hoax

Local police and volunteer fire fighting units were called out yesterday to investigate a bomb threat at the high school.

Sergeant Ron Norman said he received the threatening call at 11:35 A.M. on Sunday. Although the caller's voice sounded young and he considered that the information given was probably false, he investigated the situation, since police had a responsibility to follow up all bomb-threat calls.

The high school was thoroughly searched but no evidence of a bomb was found.

Sunday's bomb threat was the first real opportunity to use the services of Constable David Andrews since he took up duties at the Hamelin station on Friday. A second police vehicle had also been delivered.

Speaking from the Hamelin station this morning, Sergeant Norman said, "It was good to know that while I attended to matters at the school, there was still an officer available for highway patrol."

Item 25

From the Standard Weekend Edition, *Saturday/Sunday,*
August 9/10, 1986

A Murderer's Diary
The fourth installment of the
journal of Wouter Loos

This installment is translated by Professor Hans Freudenberg
and introduced by Jill Boxtel, Reader in Australian History,
Barrie College, and author of From Other Worlds: European
Children Castaways in the South Seas, 1770–1870.[1]

Since the first media release of Steven Messenger's now famous discoveries some four months ago, there is little doubt
that the possibility of the mummified human hand belonging
to a European child castaway has been one of the most interesting aspects in the case.

But if there was such a child, from what vessel was he
or she cast away? And when?

Too many questions? Possibly—yet not necessarily
without answers. History has a curious way of providing answers where and when we least expect them, and the case of
the castaway's hand may well be solved in this installment of
Loos's journal.

But let's first take a look at some other children who
have found themselves in similar predicaments.

The Historic Shipwrecks Office, based in Canberra, ac-

---

1. Festus-Williams, Sydney, 1985.

knowledges 107 shipwrecks, officially entitled "declared wrecks," in Australian waters. The earliest of these is the British East India Vessel *Trial*, which sank off Western Australia in 1622; the most recent is the Japanese submarine *1-124* off Darwin in 1944.

Today, although shipwrecks still occur, better navigational charts and instruments, plus highly efficient air-sea rescue services, mean that subsequent deaths at sea are far less frequent.

Remarkably enough, even in colonial times, many people did survive shipwrecks and often spent months at sea upon rafts or were cast up on some strange and often hostile shore to cope as best they could.

One of the earliest known cases of a white child survivor was that of Joe Forbes, of the Schooner *Stedcombe*, which was burned to the water line by natives off the island of Timor in 1823. At the age of ten years, Joe was claimed by native inhabitants of Timor as "a child returned from the dead," and so began a period of exile lasting sixteen years. When rescued by a visiting schooner, the *Essington*, on March 31, 1839, Forbes had virtually lost the use of his native English, could not walk as a result of confinement in a hut, and was covered in ulcerated sores. Remarkably, he retained his waistcoat and a piece of white cloth that he wore about his genitals.

Not so fortunate was John Edwards, also ten years old, who was taken captive along with Forbes. Edwards died, presumably from malnutrition, in 1835, four years before Forbes's rescue.

The story of James Wilson, an apprentice aboard the *Peruvian* wrecked off the Queensland coast on February 24, 1846, is equally tragic.

Wilson survived forty-two dreadful days upon a raft,

drifting at the mercy of the sea. Although other survivors aboard had agreed not to eat human flesh, they did use the limbs of those who died as bait, lassoing and clubbing to death the sharks that rose to take the grisly offerings. Having survived this ordeal, Wilson was also claimed as a "lost child" or "jumped-up white fellow" by native tribesmen near Mount Elliott. Wilson died among them two years later and, following tribal custom, was cremated at Port Denison. One of his fellow survivors from the *Peruvian,* James Morrell, who was twenty-two at the time of the wreck, lived with the Aborigines for seventeen years until his rescue in 1863. It was Morrell who finally told the tale of James Wilson's fate.

To this day no one knows the full story of two white girls whose dreadful experiences are tantalizingly related in the *Sydney Morning Herald* of Monday, October 17, 1859. These girls, referred to as Kitty (about fifteen or sixteen) and Maria (about six or eight), were believed to be the survivors of the *Sea Belle* which went down off Fraser Island in April 1857. Rumor among seamen was that the girls' mother also survived for a short time, but upon her death the girls were raised by Aborigines on Fraser Island until rescued by Captain Arnold of the *Coquette* on October 7, 1859. The *Sydney Morning Herald* reports that, after landing in Sydney, the girls were slowly recovering, yet

> their appearance is heartrending. Their bodies, emaciated from long suffering and exposure to the weather, are covered with a coating of hair; the skin, stained by their tormentors to assimilate with their own, has become spotted and wrinkled, as if from old age; the nose has been flattened by force, the limbs distorted, and the vacant stare of idiotcy [*sic*] has left these poor creatures scarcely human in appearance, and, although enabled

gradually to recognize such things as they must have been in the habit of seeing hourly before they fell into the hands of the natives, their acquaintance with their mother tongue is as yet apparently quite gone.

The girls' subsequent fate is equally touching. Apparently they were taken in by government authorities and educated but Kitty, the eldest, died in an institution. Maria worked in domestic service, slowly relearning her native English. She died at the Sydney hospital in 1878.

Of course there must be other children, as yet unknown, who have suffered a similar fate—but here is the story of one that, miraculously, history has chosen to reveal.

Journal entry for December 16, 1629

This is our twelfth day among the Indians. We no longer fear for our lives and grow stronger each hour spent in their care. As I write, the children are about me, they stare and call out in delight as I mark this page, wanting to touch the book and the marks themselves. Some stand beside me and, with their empty hands, write on the air. They have no understanding of what I do and if I try to teach them they laugh and run off after a short time. But later, when they play among themselves, I see that they have made my lesson a game, copying my voice and actions with great skill.

It is the same with the boy. On our second day, by which time he realized we were not to die or be eaten, he removed from the iron pot one of the wooden toys from Nüremberg. This he took to the children who played in the dust about the huts. The toy he chose was a wooden soldier, about twelve inches high, brightly painted with a red cap and coat, boldly cross-strapped in white, and with long black boots. The figure can be made to move by wires and hooks, marching and nodding its head when some of these are pulled, raising his musket and sword with others. The boy called the children to him and, working the soldier in a drill, held it out for them to see.

On the instant there were squeals of delight. Never has there been such a fuss. From around the camp other children came, then the Indians left their work to see the cause of the commotion. The boy held the soldier up, both to save it from grasping hands and to allow all to see. Then, keeping it high, and working the levers vigorously, he marched off in a circle around the camp, moving his own head and legs in the same jerking actions as the toy.

At this, a hush fell upon the Indians; warriors and children alike watched with earnest attention.

When he had done, the boy fell down in a heap, laughing heartily, but the Indians did not laugh again. Rather, they turned to each other in excited talking and, at once, here and there among them, individuals raised arms and legs in precisely the same manner as the wooden soldier—and as the boy who had worked it also.

Then the children ran to the boy and clambered upon him, demanding the toy, which again he was obliged to hold high above his head. Presently the warriors came, and they also held out their hands to inspect this curiosity, but when the boy denied them, anger appeared in their faces.

I called to him, "Quickly. Put it away," and he scrambled up, hurrying to return it to the iron pot.

I went with him, as did most of the Indians, who were ignorant of where the toy had come from, and no doubt wished to see where it was being taken. When they saw the boy raise the lid of the pot, which foolishly he had not clamped shut, there was a murmur from the crowd; inside there remained the rest of the toy figures, several articles of value, including the musket and this journal, and a quantity of the white stockings. I have no doubt that those Indians closest to the pot quite clearly saw its contents, but when the boy removed a bundle of the stockings in order to replace the toy, a screaming went up and the Indians fell back in great terror. This fear of the stockings, which we could not understand, was nevertheless valuable knowledge for us in preserving the few trade goods and other items that remained in the pot from the pilfering habits of the Indians. Indeed, the camp was still littered with the remains of numerous articles they had stolen at our first meeting.

However, from that day onward, despite their fear of the stockings, a group of Indians was always sitting around the pot, waiting for one or other of us to open it. When we did so there was always much excitement, but none dared come near, for each time the lid was replaced, we left a stocking hanging out from beneath it; thus the protection of our goods was assured.

December 20, 1629

We spend our days waiting. Each day I approach the older men, wishing to be taken beyond the camp to the North, where I believe there are ships. But no longer will these people bother with me and I fear that any ship will be long gone before I am able to reach it. I cannot go alone, and without a guide I am at the Indians' mercy.

Each day is much the same as another. We have brought the sled near to the hut in which we continue to sleep—no one else having made claim to it—and about this place we spend most of our hours, sitting playing with the children. The older members of the tribe now ignore us, or at times bring strangers who stare. If this should happen, the boy performs tricks, as a circus freak, standing on his head or rolling over, though I admit such behavior seems in no way odd to the Indians, who observe these foolish antics with the same expression as if he were to sit quietly in meditation. Even the wooden toys now bring little response; if one is shown to the children, their only interest is in who might steal it rather than the pleasure of watching it operate. Yet, strangely, around the great fire that burns in the center of the clearing at night, we see the warriors still making the moves of the soldier or one of the other toys, which the boy has shown them. These moves they practice and alter, and practice again, so that we see the movements of the soldier become those of the jolly sailor or the blacksmith at his anvil, depending on which toy has captured their fancy. We are not invited to these activities, but remain at our own fire before our hut.

Nor are we fed any longer. When first we arrived, food was brought to us, but now we must wait until all others have eaten, even the dogs, then forage for ourselves among the remains at the fireside.[2]

The creatures that are captured and devoured cannot be believed. These include the marvelous furred animals like the one I found dead in the dry river when first we landed. One of these was killed in the hunt and brought into camp where, miraculously, without bloodshed, a warrior removed from its

2. The situation Wouter Loos records here is very similar to that described by Eliza Fraser following the shipwreck of the *Stirling Castle* on K'gari (now Fraser Island) off the Queensland coast, May 23, 1836.

Having reached the shore in the tribal lands of the Kabi Kabi people, Mrs. Fraser and four other adult survivors assumed the Kabi Kabi would automatically provide food for all. This was not the case. Survivors would only be fed if they took part in tribal food gathering or other worthwhile activities.

Being too ignorant to learn Aboriginal food-gathering skills, Mrs. Fraser earned her keep by minding the Kabi Kabi children—Ed.

stomach a baby of the same type, which began immediately to hop around until it was clubbed to death and roasted along with its mother.

I should also advise travelers that this place is inhabited by dragons, some small and some great. These are gray scaled creatures with the head and tail of a serpent, yet running upon four legs and having dreadful talons. They do not breathe fire, as some falsely say, but their mouths are red inside, gaping wide to show horrible blue tongues.

Creatures such as these are seen quite near the camp, and if taken unawares by the Indians, are hastily killed with clubs then thrown into the ashes to bake. I have attempted to shoot a dragon with the musket, but I am always too clumsy to approach within firing range and the beast, sensing me nearby, quickly escapes.

The Indians also eat roots and vegetables similar to marrows, yet still I can find no evidence of cultivation of crops, nor husbandry of animals. Because of this, the daily search for food is the tribe's main activity and often they seem to go hungry or have lean fare when the hunt is poor. At such times the boy and I are left to starve.

December 23, 1629

Last night events occurred that caused us once again to fear for our lives, and this day has proved little better.

During the afternoon the boy had been so overcome by hunger that he went off alone to the fresh water ponds in search of food. Later he returned with certain bright nuts[3] and lily bulbs he declared were the same as those relished by the Indians, and having used his teeth to strip from them their

---

3. Possibly the bright orange fruit of *Macrozamia reidlei* (a species of cycad), which if eaten in its natural state is highly toxic, inducing vomiting and diarrhea—Ed.

outer covering, he proceeded to chew and swallow a variety of differing types. Some time after this, as dusk fell, I heard him moaning in the hut, and presently he stumbled out, retching in the grass nearby. At first I left him alone as we had both suffered similar responses to some of the Indians' diet, but when he repeated this behavior several times, and on each occasion his groaning became worse, I tried to offer assistance. This he refused, although I did take from him the shirt he had soiled in his retching. Shortly after, his groans turned to cries of agony and he began to defecate without control, only seeming to gain some relief from his suffering by rolling upon the sand, clutching at his stomach.

Being certain that he would die (as he was by no means fully recovered from his earlier fevers), I ran to the Indians who sat about the fire and indicated the boy's need for assistance. Some of the warriors came, standing off at a little distance to observe his plight, while others knelt among the grass alternately prodding with sticks or smelling the awful matter that passed from his body.

One of the graybeards moved close enough to touch him, although I soon realized this interest was not in the boy's well-being but in the golden ring that hung exposed upon his chest—for even as the boy bent forward to once again void the contents of his stomach, the Indian's hand moved to slip the leather loop carrying the ring from his neck. Suddenly aware of the old man's intentions, the boy sprang up and, despite his agony, snarled at the would-be-thief in awful rage, then plunged off into the darkness.

Overcome by the Indians' callous indifference, I ran among them screaming abuse, but this drew no reaction, for having satisfied their curiosity, they moved off again to continue their conversation by the fire.

With some difficulty I now forced myself to accept that

if the boy was to be helped, I remained his only hope—and having resolved to find him, I returned to our fire, withdrew a flaming brand, then set off to search the surrounding wilderness.

For possibly an hour or more I stumbled about in darkness, until, upon nearing the ponds, I heard what seemed to be the muffled sound of human voices among the reeds. Toward this I made my way, approaching silently in case I should encounter Indians unawares, when quite suddenly I came across my companion, lying peacefully on the grassy bank and apparently deeply engaged in conversation with himself.

Upon recognizing me, he attempted to rise, but this I prevented, dropping to the ground to express my delight at finding his condition obviously improved. He seemed equally pleased to see me—freely allowing me to support his head and shoulders in my arms—and again I was struck by the sudden changes in his nature: that at times he could be truly endearing, at others truly fearful.

So we sat for some time, he speaking of his suffering while I told of my efforts to find him, until, apparently weary of talk, he asked that I help him into the water to bathe, as the stench of his recent illness was heavy and sickening.

I was only too willing to comply and presently he lay back, breathing more easily upon the moonlit bank. At first we did not speak and, being certain that he would fall asleep from exhaustion, I prepared to keep him silent company until dawn, but when I saw his hand at his chest, rolling the curious ring that hung there over and over in his fingers, I decided to ask him of its origin.

He did not answer at once—possibly because of his weak condition or perhaps since he had no desire to tell me what I had asked—but after some thought he began, and I record his words here for I believe certain details may be of great importance in any future attempt by the Company to discover this country's wealth.

The ring was of fine gold, very plain, and set with a single stone, the name of which I do not know, though it was rich and red as blood. The boy had first seen it upon the hand of a Spaniard, a sailor who said it came from the tribe of the Golden Man, *El Dorado* of the Americas, where the mountains are so filled with gold that they shine in the daylight and so dazzle the eyes of the beholder that he may only approach them by the darkness of night.

Upon hearing these words I was overcome with wonder, for the mountains he described I had seen myself—and not in the far-off Americas but here, in this Southland. I recalled at once the shining mountains to the North where, without doubt, much gold and many precious gems lay waiting to be found.

I thought also of the crown I had drawn in the sand for the old Indian, and how he likewise drew, forming the outline of a ship, then pointed toward those very mountains. I believe now, of a certainty, that the vessel he drew belongs to the rich and mighty kingdom of the Shining Mountains, and if I could but reach that place, I would find wealth beyond compare.

So it was that the boy's words filled me with great desire, and as he spoke I was lost to them in my dreaming—therefore, I cannot recall him saying exactly how he acquired the ring. But assuredly once it was in his possession he was reluctant to wear it upon his hand—for which reason I suspect he came by it unjustly or by violence—and always it remained about his neck, threaded upon the thin leather thong. Finally, and this I plainly heard, he claimed the ring to be his most valued possession. I said nothing, but smiled within myself, for indeed, since he was cast away, it had become the only thing of value he could rightly call his own.

When the boy had finished I spoke to him of traveling North to where I believed we would find many jewels of like value, but such ideas seemed to hold no interest for him, and shortly, as we had lapsed into silence, he expressed the need to return to our hut.

For the remainder of that night I slept little, the thought of the mountains constantly beating in my brain, and, at first light, hearing the hunters preparing for their day's activities, I leapt up, collected the musket, ball, and shot from the iron pot, and set out to follow them.

In the night I had determined that I would earn my right to a guide, and that the musket, whose true value was as yet unknown to these Indians, might well come to my aid—if I could only demonstrate its power to kill.

The hunters walked at a leisurely enough pace through the low scrub and open grassland to the East. They took no notice of me, though they were aware of my presence, and wandered on, laughing and talking among themselves. It was cool and pleasant in the early morning and I admit to enjoying the notion of doing something purposeful; so in spite of the dreadful cuts and punctures made upon my naked feet by the many rocks and thorns over which we traveled, I observed all, especially the first clear rays of the sun falling upon the far mountains, flashing golden across the vast and open plain.

At length I noticed that the Indians had slowed considerably in their pace, pausing to talk softly and pointing in various directions. I fell in with a group of graybeards (whom I feared the least) and when they trotted off to the Southward, bending low, I attempted to do the same. Very soon we came upon the base of a steep ridge, densely covered in bushes, and here, falling upon their stomachs, the old men crept upward while I, a deal less easily, followed behind.

From the summit I looked down upon a remarkable, bowl-shaped depression in the earth, perhaps five hundred yards in diameter and fifty yards deep, within which I could clearly see many herds of the furred hopping creatures, some sitting back upon their long tails, others feeding contentedly on the lush grass.

This wonderful place provided for me a dilemma: surely it was the work of man, not nature, yet I could not believe these Indians would have the laborers, or the ability, to construct so huge a field for the husbandry of their herds. And indeed, if they had, why should it be necessary to fall into concealment, hunting and killing what was their own? As we lay waiting for the moment to attack, it came to me that this place, and these animals, must belong to another tribe, no doubt greater in number and intelligence than those among whom I had fallen. If this surmise were true, then perhaps these herds belonged to the ruler of the Shining Mountains to the North, and even now I stood within the borders of his golden land. With these thoughts in mind, I grew more determined to impress my companions in the hope that, having done so, I might gain a guide who would lead me to my goal.

Therefore, when the graybeards rose silently and crept over the edge of the ridge, intent on entering the enclosure, I followed closely behind, none preventing me, and when we had moved within musket range of the grazing creatures, before ever a spear could be thrown, I fired into the herd.

The report echoed over and over within the surrounding ridges and caused a great scattering of the beasts, but to my dismay, not one had been injured, neither were there any remaining to hunt. Within moments the savages were upon me, beating me with spears, and the musket, which had formed our only means of protection, was dashed upon rocks and smashed to pieces. I fell to the ground, certain of death, but the Indians' fury seemed brief and presently they ran off over the ridge, and I was alone.

I dragged myself up the slope and for some time lay in the shade of the bushes to recover. It seemed that I had brought great shame upon myself by my actions, and on my return to the camp (if indeed I could find my way there), it would be well if the boy and I left—without the benefit of a guide—to find the people of the North as soon as possible. This being resolved, I got up and limped back in the direction we had taken, arriving shortly before nightfall.

Once at the hut I was joyfully welcomed by the boy, who had long since given me up for lost, the savages having returned empty-handed some hours before, and we decided, over a tasteless meal of roots scavenged from the children, that if two days were allowed for the cuts to my feet and bruises from the beating to recover, then we should set off again for the North, with nothing lost. All being well, our departure from this tribe will therefore be upon the day that follows Christmas.

December 29, 1629

Before beginning to write, I read once more from my previous entry. How our hopes have changed since last I wrote. For during these Holy Days, Heaven has indeed smiled upon us, providing a gift the like of which we thought never to see again.

Though my ink runs low and cannot last much longer, and my hand shakes in the writing, I must tell of our Good Fortune and the prospects that lie before us.

Following my ill-fated hunting expedition, I rested two days about our hut, recovering from the injuries I had received in that exercise. During this time the boy was good to me, foraging for my food and staying near me as a true companion. I was surprised and yet heartened by this closer association and began to think more optimistically of sharing with him the perils that lay ahead.

However, even as we waited, it was clear to us both that with every passing hour the numbers of savages about the camp were increasing, and those brought to stand before us, staring, were faces we had never seen.

There was also a general increase of activity among the Indians, and we observed for the first time the gathering and storing of nuts, seeds, and tubers, the preparation of decorative items of feathers and beads, and above all, much obvious practicing of the actions copied from the wooden toys.

By noon on the second day[4] we knew, without doubt, that a great ceremony or tribal gathering was under way, for the hunters returned early with many carcasses, which were prepared for eating at once, and the air of excitement about the camp was intense. It was at this time that the boy once more began to express fears that we would be eaten and our limbs shared about for the benefit of the visitors, but I tried to calm his talk, assuring him that we were no longer of interest to the tribe, and indeed, if we were to be their meal, why had they returned from the hunt with more than their usual catch? Furthermore, I advised him to consider the flesh upon his miserable frame—we had grown so thin that our bodies combined could not satisfy the hunger of one cannibal, let alone the hundreds he believed to be camped around us.

And so it was that by the last light of day, as we sat before the hut discussing our forthcoming departure, a group of children came offering us victuals, and among their number appeared the one who would prove to be our salvation.

When first the food was offered—a collection of fat,

4. This would be Christmas Day, 1629—Ed.

gray-white grubs, baked in coals and held out to us on a strip
of bark—the boy laughed and signaled that he could not eat
such hideous things, but the children insisted, and to please
them he selected a smaller portion, which he tossed into his
mouth amid squeals of delight from the onlookers. Hardly
had he done this when his expression changed to one of astonishment, and spitting the food from his mouth, he began
to point toward the children, making incomprehensible
sounds. I believed him to be poisoned and accusing the culprit, but on looking where he indicated, the true cause of his
excitement was evident.

Behind the children, and taller than them by far, stood
another figure—its head and shoulders framed by the glow
of the fire. And from that head, radiating like spun gold,
shone a mass of yellow hair, the sight of which had rendered
my companion speechless. Then, as suddenly as it had appeared, the figure vanished, leaving us to doubt our own eyes.

But there was no time to discuss what had been seen,
for no sooner had the children turned from us in disgust than,
to our amazement, several warriors appeared, signaling that
we should follow them. The bodies of these Indians were
daubed and streaked in paint and feathers, rendering their
appearance frightful and, fearing their intentions, we endea-
vored to resist, the boy crawling back into the hut, while I
attempted to fend them off with my fists. Our efforts were to
no avail for, summoning reinforcements, they soon had me
overpowered and the boy dragged from hiding.

So we were led away, in utter confusion of the senses, to
face once more the prospect of a hideous death.

Our captors hurried us through the darkness of the surrounding bushes until, at some distance from the camp, we
stumbled into a circular clearing, at the center of which
blazed a mighty fire. Upon seeing this, the boy began scream-

ing in horror, accusing me of leading him to his death and cursing the Indians with every obscenity under heaven. It is doubtful that these protestations had any effect on our captors, and we found ourselves suddenly forced to the ground. By means of signs that could not possibly be misunderstood, we were instructed to remain still and observe.

As if our arrival had been expected, there now appeared in the clearing a solitary Indian, gorgeously decorated from head to toe in red and white feathers, his black skin glistening in the firelight. He began to move with a broken, stamping rhythm, his voice wailing horribly—then, as my eyes became accustomed to the glare, I saw many others, perhaps a hundred or more, decorated likewise in feathers and white markings, sitting just beyond the circle of stones. Among these were musicians who, through various instruments, produced the frightful droning sound to which the dancer moved and wailed.

Having completed two or three circuits of the fire, this awful creature dropped suddenly upon his hands and feet and, in the manner of an animal, began to move backward, dragging his hands in the earth to form parallel tracks, perhaps a yard apart, which weaved in and out, sometimes close to the great central fire, sometimes closer to the outer edge where the seated Indians likewise wailed and swayed. This behavior meant nothing to me, but when another entered, first falling upon his face to inspect these lines, and then to imitate the jerking motions of the wooden soldier, I began to understand what was being enacted before us.

One by one, a series of new dancers performed the movements of our toys, each perfectly demonstrating its special qualities, and soon, within the great ring, we saw our arrival in this land recreated for the entertainment of all— and the Indians' uproar was their sign of approval.

I cannot describe all I witnessed, for this ceremony lasted some hours, but when at length it seemed the frenzy of the dancers and the chanting from the onlookers could rise no higher, into the dying firelight there leaped one further creature, the like of which I pray never to see again. Two phantom limbs, white and skeletal, now pranced about the circle in a horrible mimicry of walking, yet try as I might to discern the body that moved them, none was to be seen—and a terrible hush fell—the silence of great fear.

"White stockings," the boy breathed in my ear, but I did not wait to see more.

Touching his arm as a sign for him to follow, I slipped away into the darkness, leaving the savages to whatsoever hideous apparition should materialize next.

Even after sunrise the following morning the camp remained quite still, the Indians no doubt deep in sleep from their activities of the night before. Having thus been provided with the ideal opportunity to escape unnoticed, the boy and I resolved to gather from about the camp whatever we could find of the stolen trade goods, then take our leave as quickly as possible.

The scavenging exercise completed and, thankfully, the boy having recovered our towing rope, I had just slipped into the sled's harness when I heard him whisper from behind me. "Wouter," and turned to look. There, amid low bushes not twenty yards distant, stood a pale-skinned girl, her hair golden in the morning light.

No words could express our astonishment and we stood, mute, while she continued to study us for some minutes. Slowly, then, without wishing to alarm her, I lowered the harness ropes from my shoulders and, motioning to the boy, we moved away several paces in the direction of our hut.

At this the girl came forward, leaving the protection of the bushes, and headed toward the sled. The boy glanced at me, but I did not attempt to prevent her, and presently she was touching the ropes I had dropped, the sled itself, and finally the iron pot, mounted so grandly upon it. She behaved with considerable caution, yet when she saw the stocking, which we had left hanging from the pot's lid, her manner changed. First stroking the white fabric with her finger, she then lifted the stocking to her face, rubbing it upon her cheeks and lips.

As she was so engaged, the boy and I observed her body, all the while speculating, in low tones, upon her marvelous appearance and possible origin—but of neither could we make any sense save that she must belong to a visiting tribe and was, without doubt, the same golden-haired creature we had glimpsed standing behind the children the previous night.

She stood about five feet tall and appeared healthy though quite thin. Her age may have been fifteen years or a little older, I could not tell at that time, for although she was obviously white and no Indian, her skin was darkened by exposure and grime, which clung to the animal fat these Indians rubbed upon their bodies.

Upon her head grew a tangle of unruly yellow hair, this being caught up here and there in what appeared to be lumps of gum or clay, as if some attempt had been made to control its otherwise unkempt state. The shape of her face was fine and feminine, her mouth small and well formed and, despite a downcast slant to her brows (perhaps a habit to protect herself from the sun's glare, or the constant crawling of flies), her eyes were of the liveliest blue and excited great attention against her tawny skin.

Finally, about her narrow waist she wore a girdle of plaited grasses from which hung a small piece of hide to conceal her womanhood, but all else, including her fine breasts and buttocks, was unashamedly open to our gaze.

It was a truly curious thing that during our period of observation she did not appear at all afraid, yet when the boy could contain himself no longer and stepped forward to touch her, she dropped the stocking and drew back, wary of his motives, and I gripped his arm, forcing him behind me.

In our language I said, "We are Dutchmen. Shipwrecked. Who are you?" Startled, she looked from myself to the boy.

Her fingers moved uncertainly upon her lips, then she opened her mouth wide, showing her tongue, but no words followed, only a series of hideous grunts similar to those of an animal.

At this, the boy said, "Is she a lunatic? Are her senses gone?"

Yet hardly had he spoken than the sounds came again and this time, among the nonsense, I clearly heard the word "England."

"Not lunatic," I said, "but English. She has lost her language."

And so it proved, for in a sudden rush came "Harry" (which I took to be the name of the greatest English king), then "home" and "mother," followed by other words of English (which I am incapable of writing) until, in a state of great emotion, she pressed her hands several times against her face crying, "Ela! Ela! Ela"—a word I understood to be her name.[5]

---

5. A note about names:

Loos assumes that the name Harry refers to the English king, Henry VIII (1491–1547). It seems improbable, however, that the girl would use his name to identify her nationality (particularly since she has already said "England"). It is perhaps more likely that it was the name of a member of her family, since she goes on to mention "home" and "mother."

The word "Ela" is also of interest. It may have its derivation in an English name such as Ella, Helen, or Pamela, or it might, as a contraction, have been a pet name used by the girl's family. It is possible, too, that it was all she could remember of her English name after years of isolation, or that it was not her name at all, but a word of greeting or warning, misinterpreted by Loos—Ed.

Now, although my knowledge of English was limited to what I had gleaned in taverns and aboard ships, I realized at once that if I could only converse with this girl I might gain news of other peoples who inhabited the land and learn more of the wealth I believed it promised. With this purpose in mind, I remained where I was, yet began to recite, over and over, each of the few words of the English language known to me—using at all times the gentlest tone I could contrive—until presently I saw her grow calmer, lifting her hand to once again fondle the stocking, and shaping her mouth in simple mimicry of my own.

I swear the boy thought me to be a lunatic also, but when I moved slowly forward, still speaking all the while, I sensed his presence behind me and guessed he had realized my intentions. In this manner we crossed the space separating our hut and the sled and presently stood face-to-face with the girl, only the sled itself and the iron pot upon it coming between us.

I now confess that having accomplished so much and being no more than a yard from the girl herself, my English babble suddenly failed me, leaving only silence.

But even as I stood, certain that our sole hope would run off in terror at any moment, her hand left the stocking and reached out above the pot.

Both the boy and myself drew back on the instant, ceasing to breathe, yet still the hand came and in a moment I saw its purpose—about the boy's neck, exposed and glinting in the morning light, hung the golden ring.

No sooner had her fingers touched him, lifting the ring from his chest, than the boy began to speak.

"It is a ring," he said softly in our own tongue. "It is a golden ring. But pretty as you are, you cannot have it. Not this lovely thing."

And he went on, his eyes never once leaving her face. I

knew, even then, that we had at last found the one who would save us.

So it was that we met Ela, and although little more was gained from that meeting—for she ran off at the first sign of life from the awakening camp—the boy begged that we remain, allowing him time to know her better. With this reasoning I could hardly argue, for what other hope did we have? None at all—not maps, nor weapons, nor food, nothing.

And thus, on New Year's Day, still seated before my hut, I conclude this entry.[6]

The boy is once again off with Ela, but I do not mind this solitude, for each day in her company he seems to grow stronger, learning more of her and her people. When the time comes for the tribes to return to their various territories, it is my belief we shall travel with hers to the North.

This concludes the fourth installment of the Loos journal.

Item 26

Letter to the Editor, the Standard, *Wednesday, August 13, 1986*

Sir,

What a great thrill it was to share the experiences of the mysterious Ela, the English girl castaway, in your latest extract from Wouter Loos's diary.

Regrettably I cannot say I was equally impressed by the

---

6. New Year's Day, 1630. This section has taken four days to record—Ed.

quality of the article on child castaways by Jill Boxtel that introduced the piece.

While I have no doubt that Ms. Boxtel's research into European children cast away in the South Pacific must be extensive, she would do well to tell the whole story in each case she discusses.

Unfortunately for Ms. Boxtel, I have also researched the fate of the two white sisters, Kitty and Maria, who Ms. Boxtel claims were rescued after being cast away on Fraser Island in 1859.

That entire story is pure fabrication and a cruel hoax. I would like to set the record straight for the benefit of your readers.

In 1859 the schooner *Coquette,* under the command of a certain Captain Arnold, was sent out at the request of the New South Wales government to rescue two white females presumed cast away on Fraser Island. On arrival, Captain Arnold and Mr. Sawyer, the owner of the *Coquette,* found the girls to be two remarkably pale-skinned Aboriginal sisters, named Mundi and Coyeen, natives of the area, living peacefully with their Aboriginal parents. However, since Sawyer had been offered three hundred pounds to bring back two "white" girls, that is exactly what he did—the fact that they were kidnapped, not "rescued," meant nothing to him.

This frightful situation explains why the little girls were so terrified when they reached Sydney, why they could not speak English, why their noses appeared to have been broken, why their skin was so "stained"—they were Aboriginal children who had been stolen away.

The "institution" where Mundi (renamed Kitty) died was in fact an insane asylum, while Coyeen (Maria) was forced to work as a housemaid for the very people who had so cruelly kidnapped her.

There are many such instances of black child kidnappings by whites (all for the "right" reasons, of course) and I often wonder if anyone will ever bother to write a book about them—or will they remain as they are now, no more than footnotes to history?

Christine Bundalil
McKenna Station
Alice Springs

Item 27

Messenger, Midway Roadhouse

From the time Kratz took me down to the mission I was very unsettled. My chest pains came back, and my fever. There were also more dreams.

I remember one in particular, early in the week. When I woke up there was blood on my hand, as if the ring had ripped at my finger and cut me. That dream didn't start like a dream. I could see Steven Messenger under the motel sign, but then it went very different. While he was waiting, and hitching with his thumb the way he did sometimes, this rig pulled up. It was massive but it couldn't be seen, only the front wheel and bumper were there, then the door swings open, and Steven Messenger steps off the highway, onto the running board, and into the cab. For a split second, before the door shuts, there is his hand and the ring is on his finger, very clear. Then the door shuts. There is a luminous yellow of dashlights, the deep rhythmic throb-throb of engine noise, and the white line of the highway blurring into darkness.

But across the seat, from the driver's side, comes this

other hand—it's not a man's hand or a woman's—it's more like a skeleton hand, or a five-fingered claw, and it's crawling very slowly over the seat. Steven Messenger doesn't know, but it's heading straight for him, for his hand with the ring, which is resting right there on the seat beside him. Then the five-fingered claw touches him and he is screaming, because this thing has grabbed him around the wrist, while another just like it is working at his fingers, tearing off the ring, and he is screaming and screaming.

One thing about having a dream was that I would wake up, and it would be over, and everything was all right.

But the dreams weren't all that worried me. Outside my window there seemed to be tracks or footprints in the sand, as if somebody had been standing there, looking in. I went out several times to check on these and sometimes they were there, sometimes they weren't, as if a trick was being played.

It got so bad I couldn't tell what was real, exactly.

When I was upset like that and needed to calm down, I usually worked some more on the Life Frame. The Frame itself was nearly finished; it only needed some sort of base and, of course, a specimen.

It was most important that the creature I chose for this purpose (that is, the thing to actually be encased in the Frame) was free of injury and perfect in every way. This was to make sure the skeleton itself would be perfect. I therefore needed to immobilize the specimen instantly and permanently, so that, once fitted, it did not thrash around and damage itself on the wire. Of course, I had taken great care with the knotting. There were no rough or jagged edges.

The radio aerial Kratz had thrown in the trash came in handy here. I was very interested in this and spent a long time lying on my bed working it in and out as I had seen Kratz do. There were three chromed metal sections left, each sliding neatly into the next. I eventually got rid of the two bottom sections, which were hollow, and kept only the top one. This was a solid metal rod, very thin, with a small knob at one end, something like a knitting needle. (Possibly a knitting needle would have done, but my mother did not own one.)

In the afternoons, I went to the part of the cliffs where the wind had exposed the flat rock of the edge. I took a bottle of water and got down on my knees to work the rock as a whetstone, honing the rod to the finest point. I was not worried about how long this took, or the time.

Once I was still working into the night. By moonlight the metal was fantastic, like a beam of thin silver. I could picture it as a photo in *Popular Science* with a caption: "Man made: the perfect artefact."

Of course, I still had to choose the specimen itself. For weeks I had given this a lot of thought, off and on. From a book on reptiles in the Shire Council Library, I had removed a few pages detailing the anatomy of lizards. I was very interested in the illustrations of internal organs and bone structure and made sketches of these myself. I had plenty of time to compare this theoretical information with the real thing— the sleek, silvery-gray blue-tongue lizard that impressed me as the most worthwhile specimen squatted every day on the same rock I had used to prepare the rod.

Behind its front leg, but above the rib cage, was a curious soft spot, a pulsing sack of leathery skin that most times was the reptile's only sign of life.

It was this sack I intended to penetrate, lying flat on my stomach like the lizard itself, and running the rod over my fingers, like the movement of a billiard cue, to pierce the skin at the precise point of contact where the needle tip, sliding home, could prick the heart.

So that's how I kept myself busy. I suppose some people,

under the same pressure as I was, would have gone to bed and stayed there. But I wasn't like that. I never missed a day of school that week, and every morning and afternoon I sat in the bus next to Kratz. Even when he told me that he had worked up the nerve to go back down the mission to trade some kerosene for one of their car seats, I never flinched. It seemed Kratz would risk anything for his Dream Machine. But when he asked me to help fit the seat, so it would be better for his "mate," Charlie, to sit on going up the ranges, that's when I drew the line. I said it had been all right for me to have the wires sticking up my butt. Naturally, being Kratz, he thought that was funny.

I think if the ring had been performing properly I would have felt better. But there was the worry with that too. Sure, there was no doubt in my mind that it was mine. I had no trouble with that public ownership thing anymore, not since the time it lit up, glowing, in my dresser. I knew that was a sign. But while it still felt warm to me, and comfortable (most times), nothing was happening like before. There were no flights, so to speak.

There were certain changes in the other Steven Messenger as well. On the Friday morning I woke up very early. It was hardly light, but I thought I could hear a wheezing sound outside my window. It was the sound I make when there is phlegm in my chest. I looked out quickly and I could see Steven Messenger, from the back, standing inside the fence of our property, maybe two yards from the window. He had his bedroll, etc.

But when he turned, as if he knew I was watching, there was no face. Well, certainly not his movie face, with flesh and skin. This was the shape of a face, but empty, except for two gray hollows for eyes, like the eyes of a cave fish. Then he was gone.

I looked for tracks in the sand, or marks where he came under the fence from the Roadhouse side, but there was nothing.

I got so depressed I went straight down the cliff edge and used the rod. The specimen was lying there in the morning sun and I killed it, just like that. I knew I had to do something.

I picked the specimen up with my bare hands and put it in a shoe box. I carried it back to the trailer and slipped it under my bed, where it was cool. My timing was okay. I could place it on the ants' nests early on the Saturday and have the whole day to watch.

Then I had a shower and scrubbed myself in time for school.

Item 28

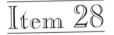

Photocopied from

The Unexplained:
A Dictionary of Terms from Legend and
the Supernatural*

El Dorado: The Spanish term *El Dorado* literally means "the Golden One" or "the Golden Man." The term was first used by European conquistadors of the 15th and 16th centuries who searched for the fabled "tribe of the golden man" which they believed existed deep in the South American jungle.

In ancient times there was a pre-Columbian tribe whose chief ceremonially rolled in gold dust then dived into a sacred lake, but these people had perished long before the arrival of the Spaniards.

Nevertheless, the legend of El Dorado continued to grow. Some believed it to be a city paved in gold, others a mountain of crystal blinding to the naked eye.

El Dorado was never found, but today its mystery lives on as a symbol for every goal beyond attainment; every dream beyond reality.

*Marginal drawings by Steven Messenger, labeled as the Centralian blue-tongue lizard *(Tiliqua multifasciata)*—Ed.

Item 29

Messenger, Midway Roadhouse

Coming home on the bus that Friday afternoon Kratz said, "Are you all right for tomorrow?"

I said "What?" Because on the Saturday I was taking the Life Frame with the specimen up to the headland ant nests. I had managed to pick up a very nice magnifying glass from the science room and was going to use it for this purpose.

He said, "Going up the ranges, moron." (I always remember him talking to me like that.)

"That's Sunday," I said. "That's what we worked out with Charlie."

I admit Kratz said he was sorry, and that it was a genuine mistake, but he hadn't told me the day had been changed. There was some Abo wingding on that Sunday. Charlie had told Kratz when he went to pick up the seat for the pickup.

So I said, "Okay. What time?"

He said about 9 o'clock and I told him I'd be ready, but I was thinking I would have to chuck the specimen. I couldn't leave it under my bed all day Saturday. It would get rotten in the heat.

But things turned out quite differently.

For the second morning in a row I was woken up very early by the wheezing. This time the face without eyes was right at the window and I could see it was not me, at least not the other Steven Messenger, though similar—the clothes, etc.

I said, "You'd better go away. I am the owner now."

I meant the ring, of course, and he seemed to understand and turned and vanished.

I was very pleased with the way I behaved, but after that there was no hope of going back to sleep and it was only 5 A.M. I thought that, instead of lying there doing nothing, I might as well try an experiment, so I got dressed, put the specimen with the Life Frame in my backpack and walked up to the nests.

I was back by 6:30 and over at the garage by 8 o'clock. I felt good. Scrubbed up, breakfasted, and not a bit worried about the day. That old bastard Sunrise could do or say what he liked.

When Kratz turned up I said, "Hi there. How's the Dream Machine? Ready to roll?"

He said, "Jeez, Messenger, did you get lucky, or have you been enjoying yourself at that motel peephole?"

He could never accept me being friendly. He always had to bring me down. But I didn't care. I said that to myself.

He put a cooler chest in what he called his survival kit, the tool box fitted to the truck bed, then he put his stupid goggles on and we left. My mother hadn't got up, so she didn't know where I went.

I have to admit it never entered my head that Charlie might have forgotten we were coming; at least, I never mentioned that possibility until we were nearly at the mission. But Kratz shook his head.

"No way," he said. "That old fella was busting to get to those ranges."

Then he looked across the cab, "And he especially wants to go with you—I'm just the stooge providing the transport."

"Like a chauffeur," I said, and started laughing.

Outside the mission Kratz ran the pickup into the bushes where he had left it before and headed off through the cemetery. I waited. He hadn't gone a hundred yards when out of the gravestones came Charlie, right out of nowhere.

"Okay. I'm here," he said. "I'm ready." He had what looked like a bag of groceries under his arm, but when Kratz went to take it to put it in the tool box with the cooler chest, he wouldn't let go and said it stayed with him.

There was also a problem with where we were going to sit. Kratz said it was best Charlie was in the middle, next to him, so he could hear him give directions over the wind. That meant I was up against the door with Charlie's filthy pants rubbing on mine and his twisted hand nearly touching me.

(I should mention that it was then, in the sunlight, that I noticed his skin was not black, but more a green-black, a color like the ants at the mission. This is what people call an iridescent green.)

About three or four miles up the highway was an unmarked dirt road heading northeast and Charlie said to turn there. Kratz seemed happy to do that; although this road wasn't much more than a sandy track, there was no chance of running into the highway patrol—or anybody else for that matter. He said, "How far along here do we go?" but Charlie just moved one twisted-up hand forward a few times.

"I'll say when we get there," he said, so we didn't speak then.

We passed through the usual low scrub, the same as around the Roadhouse, but I felt as if we were climbing all the time, and finally, after about half an hour, I knew I was right. The truck broke through the bushes at the top of a ridge and all at once, right in front of me, appeared this amazing landscape. The ground seemed to sink in one huge crater, its dead flat surface a shimmering lake of glass, and on this, or above it, danced a range of dazzling hills, flashing back light rays that hit my eyes like mirrors, blinding me, so

I was forced to cover my face with my hands and turn away.

Kratz stopped the pickup.

He looked across and said, "What's up, Stevo? Your future too bright for you?" and he chucked over another pair of goggles. (He was still wearing his.)

With the goggles on I was able to look up. I guessed what I was seeing, the pan of a salt lake and the ranges beyond it reflecting the sun—but it seemed different from that, not from this world, fantastic. Charlie sat staring straight out into it, like he was hypnotized. The glare didn't worry him, maybe because he was half blind anyway.

Then we went down, the red dust changing into a narrow track across the broken surface, and sticking out at us were wedges and slabs of the gray-white salt, forced upward from the earth.

Maybe it was the quiet, or the effect of the light, but I started to feel a sort of dreaminess (I'm sure I didn't go to sleep), the next thing we were flying straight off the edge of the salt pan and onto another track with boulders all around, so I guessed we were at the base of the range.

I saw Kratz push his goggles up, and did the same myself, then he was saying, "Look, Charlie, I have to know. I've been driving over an hour—forty, fifty miles. How much farther? It's the gas."

He tapped the dash, and I saw the cracked glass on the gauge. "We're about half empty already. And I don't even know if this thing is accurate."

Charlie straightened up then. He grinned a little. From the side I could see his teeth.

"Nearly there," he said. "Can't go much farther in this thing anyway."

About five minutes later, we saw he was right—the track just ended, ran itself into a sheer rock wall, about sixty yards high. There wasn't any choice. Kratz had to stop.

Charlie said, "Okay."

Then straight off he leaned across me to open the door, and I had to pull back against the seat. His sweaty hair was right in my face.

Kratz said, "Hang on. That one's busted. This side."

He was already getting out and Charlie went after him. I wasn't so fast, my legs were cramped from being up against the door and I had pins and needles in my feet. Outside, I heard Charlie talking to himself—or maybe to Kratz—like instructions I couldn't understand.

By the time I crawled out, Kratz was behind a boulder and he yelled over his shoulder. "Follow Charlie. He shot through. I can't stop now." I guessed what Kratz was doing and went up a track between the rocks.

I knew Charlie didn't have any shoes on, I had seen his feet in the truck, but the ground was covered in little orange pebbles and since it sloped up, I couldn't get any grip. I think maybe his toes (twisted and horny like they were) could dig in, because after a couple of minutes slipping and crawling on my hands and knees I lost him, and Kratz was coming up behind me.

He said, "Jeez, Messenger. I drive you all this way and what do you do? Lose the damn guide!"

I turned around and looked at him. My chest was starting to ache and my hands were covered in orange dirt. Already I didn't feel so good. I could feel my face getting hot.

"I'm not the one who took a leak," I said. "That's how come he's gone. So don't start on me, okay?"

He shut up after that and sat on the track. I leaned against a rock to catch my breath and tried to get my hands clean.

Then he said, "Well, anyway, I'm going back. I need a

cold drink and something to eat. He'll be back too. He's left his grocery bag in the truck."

He slid down the track on his backside, but I went down hand over hand against the rock wall. Then we got the cooler chest out and tried to have some lunch. The flies were terrible, all over the food, in our mouths, ears, and eyes. Kratz took the goggles out of the truck and wore them while he ate, but I ended up putting the food away. That was when I saw Charlie's bag. I got it out and emptied it on the truck bed.

There were a few bits of hard clay stone, yellow and red, a few empty glass bottles, only small like mustard jars, and some pieces of stick, covered in paint, the same orange as the rocks, then, one thing, a piece of quartz crystal, the best I had ever seen. It was at least four or five inches long and about one and a half or two inches across. I held it to the light and it was perfect—clear right through, not clouded or cracked anywhere. It was heavy and cold. Kratz put out his hand to take it. He held it up to the light too, but this time it caught the sun and a rainbow flashed across his face. I took it back then and put it against my face because it was so cold and smooth, but Kratz was watching.

He said, "I think that better go in the bag, not your pocket," and took it from me to put back with the rest of the stuff.

It was times like that Kratz really got on my nerves. But I didn't say anything.

After that we looked around for a while, in among the boulders, until Charlie turned up. His face looked crazy.

"Okay," he said. "Okay. I found it now. It's been a long time."

Kratz looked at me and grinned as if to say, "Here we go," then next thing, Charlie asked where his bag was, and took off.

He went up the same track as before and we followed, working from rock to rock until the little pebbles were gone and we could walk easily. All the while Charlie was talking to himself, and sometimes looking back to see if I was following. We went on like that for twenty minutes or so, until the path leveled out and there were no more boulders, only the vertical walls of a canyon, a great rip in the side of the mountain itself. The sun died, leaving everything in shadow, very cool and still. Charlie's voice echoed off the solid walls, and behind me nearly in my ear, I could hear Kratz breathing.

I didn't like the place, but I kept on going until Charlie stopped and turned around, his face still crazy, splotched and gray, as if all the blood had run out of him. He was standing in front of a solid rock wall that dripped green and black with slime.

Right away I thought this was a setup, that he had led us into this dead end to get rid of us, and I remember grabbing the ring under my shirt. But he started talking, and his eyes were so wide open I could see the blood and veins inside.

". . . Things you see . . ." he was saying, ". . . you never tell . . . you shut your mouth . . . Okay? . . . Okay?"

I nodded and Kratz did the same, then next thing Charlie was gone, straight into the rock.

Kratz pushed his hands against the slime. "Here," he said, and his arm disappeared, then his shoulder, then his head and the rest of his body. I had to do the same or else I would have lost him. I put my hand out but the green wasn't really slime, it was a sort of soft fern and gave way under my fingers. I held my breath and pushed into it and found I could move through it the same as the others had.

Inside was the narrowest fissure in the rock, hardly a body width across. My face was pressed against one wall and my shoulder blades grazed the other. My arms were spread wide, hands and fingers groping for direction.

Up front I heard Kratz say, "Keep going. Charlie's here near me."

So I went on, hoping to hell nothing revolting turned up on the rock too near my face.

I was sure I would suffocate. My chest was terrible. I couldn't get my breath and my ribs were tight, like they would crack. Under my hands and in my fingernails was black slime, but I had to keep going because to stop would be worse.

Then the cleft gradually widened and I could turn my head to see Kratz and Charlie at the far end, silhouetted against the bright light of day.

The place we came into was an enclosure about thirty yards in diameter, surrounded on all sides by cliffs rising seventy or eighty yards—but what made it so strange was that the cliffs leaned inward and the opening to the sky was like a disk of white light right up above.

Looking up made my head spin. I had to reach out and touch the walls, or else I would have fallen over.

Kratz stood opposite me, across a pool of dark water, and he was saying over and over, "Oh, jeez. Oh, jeez," and shaking his head.

When he saw me he said, "This is a sinkhole, a dirty big hole worn into the solid rock by a boulder rolling around on it, grinding down into it for a million billion years. That boulder was probably worn away to a pebble when the dinosaurs were little."

We sat for a while, looking around, and watching Charlie. He was going around the walls, talking to himself. Once or twice I saw him dig into his bag and take something out, but I couldn't really tell what he was doing.

"He's touching up the artwork," Kratz said. "That's how

come all those paints were in his bag. Poor old bastard. Must be some special place for him."

Right then, Charlie called me. He said, "Hey, you," as if I didn't have a real name.

Kratz shoved me in the ribs. "That's you, Stevo. This must be the big one. The meaning of it all. Go on," and he shoved me again.

I went around the pool and over to where Charlie was waiting. He made an arc with his arm to show me the stone walls.

"See," he said. "You can see it all now. Midday. Only time the sun comes clear over the top."

I looked. The direct light of the sun flooded the floor and walls of the cavern, driving straight down the giant shaft.

". . . Here," he was saying, "this is why I came." His crooked hand was moving over the face of the rock. "See?"

But at first I couldn't see anything—until Kratz came up behind me and reached around to grab the wrist of my right hand. I pulled away, but he forced me until my hand pressed flat against the rock.

"There," he said and did it again, "and there . . . and . . ."

Then I saw. Over and over, everywhere, were hundreds of hand prints, very pale and faded, white and yellow and red all over the wall. This place was an art gallery. There were sea creatures and animals as well: dugongs, sharks, a whale, wallabies, lizards, and a few even done in what is called the X-ray style where bones and internal organs are visible (very like sketches I had made myself of the Life Frame specimen).

But all this was nothing special and I was wondering why it was so important for me to come, when Charlie grabbed my shirt and whispered, "Here," right in my face.

I figured he was trying to show me something without Kratz.

I thought, "Okay, now maybe I can find out what this is all about and get it over with."

We had been working our way around the walls—clockwise, that is—and if the narrow fissure where we came in was 6 o'clock, then at that moment Charlie and I stood at about 2 o'clock. Kratz had gone back into the center, just staring around. Charlie took me on, maybe another ten yards, to a place where the rock walls changed. Instead of rising straight up from the floor and then leaning inward, like they did everywhere else, here they went up three or four yards then jutted out to form a sort of awning or ledge maybe six or seven yards wide. When we got beneath this and stopped, he reached into his bag and pulled out the crystal. He took a good grip with his shaky hand and pointed up.

It was dark and hard to see under there, in the shadow, so at first I thought he was just showing me the formation, but then my eyes adjusted and what I saw made me feel sick.

Using the diamond point of the crystal, he was tracing over the designs that appeared on the underside of the ledge. These weren't anything like those around the rest of the walls, not painted directly on to the rock, but scratched into it and, where paint had been used, this was very bright, as if it had been put on only the day before.

But none of that was the problem. I didn't care about how this stuff had been done. It was *what* the shapes were that made me sick—and the thought of who made them— because I could see straight off that no black man had made this. These marks were made by a white person—probably a white kid—exactly the same kind of drawing I did in first grade. Except, when I looked at the story they told, jumbled up as it was, I knew right away who the artist was—and Charlie knew I would, too.

I could see ships, old sailing ships, and wriggling lines to show waves. In the waves was a girl or woman with breasts, and a baby next to her, and her hair floating out from her head, the yellow paint still in the scratches. Along from this was a sled, very clear, with a circular shape on it (the cannibal pot, I guessed) and around, farther from that, what I thought were white boomerangs—hundreds of them—painted all over.

But the most impressive paintings of all were of two stick figures, just off to the side, with giant sunny faces, their eyes round and wide, and their mouths curved up smiling. One of these was shown much bigger than the other. The little one seemed to be wearing pants. But the big one was amazing. He had no clothes and there was no doubt he was a he. His legs were wide apart, his arms were raised high, as if he was doing a star jump. He was smiling, as I said, and around his white hair was yellow paint, like a halo, and I saw one hand, the right one, had scratched on its little finger the circle of a ring.

My chest and face were burning, and when Charlie pointed up the back, in one of the darkest places, I was sure I would faint. Right in front of me, picked out in the rock, were the letters I knew well. ELA again and again. ELA.

In my ear I heard him say, "You know her. Hey. You know all about her, and you know him too, the little fellow."

He was pointing to the smaller figure with the pants.

Then he came back, to my face, his breath all over me. "And the big one. Him with the white hair and the light around his head. See the ring. That's you, the pale one who walks at night."

Before I could do anything he reached up and ripped the

leather off my neck, the ring leather, and it snapped so the ring bounced onto the rock.

I can't say what happened after that, not for sure.

I know I fell on the rocks after the ring and got it on my hand. The burning was so bad in my face and head that my hair was like fire. There was also the grinning mouth of Charlie and his teeth, I can picture that, then his body, green, iridescent, as I said before.

But I got rid of him. I hit him with the back of my hand. He was nothing, only bones. I heard his skull crack against the rocks.

And then I was outside in the light, or the shaft of light.

I can remember Kratz being there, he is in this picture, pointing to the wall, to the rock with the star man and the white boomerang things, and a voice saying, "White stockings, the white stockings," which could have been me (my own voice), but I was going up by that time, through the air into the sky and the pure bright light and after that, a blank.

Item 30

From the Standard Weekend Edition,
Saturday/Sunday, August 16/17, 1986

A Murderer's Diary
The fifth installment of the journal of Wouter Loos

Translated and introduced by Professor Hans Freudenberg

One of the most rewarding aspects of my work on the Loos journal was a wonderful trip to the Murchison District that the *Standard* so generously provided for me in early June.

Seeing at first hand the desolate coastline that Loos and Pelgrom followed was certainly an unforgettable experience, as
was my visit to Hamelin, where I met some of the people who
had been instrumental in the discovery of the iron pot and
who had taken part in the subsequent investigations into the
origin of the journal.

In this regard, I consider myself particularly fortunate to
have met Senior Sergeant Ron Norman, the police officer
who played such a vital role in assisting Hope Michaels during the early days of the investigation. It was through Sergeant Norman and his close association with the Murchison
District Aboriginal Council that I was introduced to the remarkable Charles Sunrise, one of the Council Elders.

Charlie (as he prefers to be called) has an encyclopedic
knowledge of Aboriginal lore, and it is this attribute,
matched by his ability to spin this knowledge into stories,
that has endeared him to so many of the researchers on the
project. I regret that my stay in Hamelin could not be ex-
tended so that Charlie and I might have shared one more cup
and had the chance to talk a good deal longer.

It was during one of our sessions that I asked Charlie to
explain to me the significance of the whale in Aboriginal cul-
ture, as this issue was of the utmost importance to an understanding of the section of Loos's journal that forms this fifth
installment. Although I had succeeded in translating the section concerned, I had to admit that its true meaning remained
a mystery to me. I record Charlie's response here as, without
it, many readers (like myself in the first instance) may make
little sense of a major section of this installment. This is what
Charlie said:

> For you people, for white people, these whales only
> mean money. The whites kill the whales for oil, a terrible

thing. They spear them from ships and cut them up alive. These things I have seen, many years ago. When I was a boy, up north in Broome.

But for my people, the blacks, this whale is not an animal, he is a person like me. Yes, he is a person. He comes into the low water, where it's shallow, and he makes spray—he is the rainmaker—and then he makes the rainbow.

But sometimes this fella he gets so busy making the rain he forgets where he is, and the water runs out, the tide, and he finds himself up there on the beach, stuck there. This is okay; it's a good thing. Then he has a long visit with me, with my people who are his friends. He stays until his body changes, his whole body changes, and he makes a place, a Dreaming Place. Then everybody is happy—all us blacks are happy.

But they don't come so much anymore, these big fellas, they don't visit much nowadays. I look out from up on the cliff, in a place I go up there, but everything is changed, and they don't come anymore.

It is a wonderful thing to compare Charlie's words with those of Wouter Loos, that faltering European, trying so desperately to come to terms with the enigmatic Southland. And even as we read we may well think of the ancient prophet Jonah, emerging from the belly of his mighty whale—and of Pelgrom, only a boy, but no less a harbinger of doom.

Journal entry dated January 7, 1630

Three or four days after the completion of the great dancing ceremonies, Ela came to the boy with the news that her people would be returning North. This was the opportunity for which we had waited; the boy being eager for any further chance to be in her company while I still dared hope that she might guide us to the Shining Hills.

The day of our departure, however, was in no way remarkable. Had I waited for some grand farewell, or tearful leave-taking, I should still be there to this day. Indeed, it was difficult to tell that the tribe was intending to travel at all, and had not the girl come to our hut, signing that we make haste, we would never have known her people had left—for while we must either drag or push the sled and its cargo, the Indians simply gathered up their weapons and baskets, then proceeded to wander off in what appeared to be a most disorderly fashion.

The route taken generally followed the coastline, yet, unlike ourselves in earlier travels, the Indians did not walk upon the beach but in the sandhills, or low scrub, adjacent to the shore. Here, I now discerned, were meandering pathways—similar to tracks made by cattle in their seemingly aimless wandering among the fields at home. I was also made aware of the advantages of this route; as the majority of tracks were elevated upon the sandhills, they caught the prevailing breeze from the sea, which both served to keep us cool in our exertions and also drove away the swarms of flies that otherwise settled upon our bodies in vile black masses. Furthermore, the elevation also allowed a clear view of the sea shore and the hinterland, so that at any time the Indians might choose the best offerings—whether of food or shelter—from either side of their path.

These days of travel were a great pleasure to me, and although I followed quite some distance behind the Indians, I was not excluded from their number, as often one or more of the children would walk with me, keeping up a constant (though unintelligible) gabble. The boy likewise seemed happier than ever before. He spent little time in my company, and often an entire day would pass without my seeing him. While this meant I was obliged to take the burden of the sled alone—the Indians never once offering any service in this regard—it nonetheless pleased me to see the boy cheerful and apparently forgetful of the fear that he might be roasted alive.

From what I could see, and the little he told me, much of his day was spent with Ela and two or three female Indians about her age. Mostly they played in the shallow water, chasing and splashing one another, laughing all the while, or at times they gathered mussels, crabs, and other edible life forms from the sea and shoreline.

It was as a result of such an occasion that the boy returned to me, panting in great excitement, and holding out an object for my inspection. At first sight the repulsive thing that lay in his palm, glistening vilely, bore the appearance of human feces and, assuming this to be one of his foolish jokes, I pushed him from me in disgust. Yet, even as I did so, his hand squeezed shut and from between his fingers oozed a dark fluid that trickled down his forearm and dripped from his elbow, staining the sand at our feet with the loveliest shade of purple.

"This is a slug," he said. "The sea is filled with them. They squirt the purple juice so that they may hide in the colored water it makes," and, allowing the revolting creature to slip from his grasp, he held out his palm, to show the dark fluid cupped there. "I brought it for you, Wouter. You see. It is like ink."

I could have hugged him. Dropping the harness at once I opened the pot to remove my inkwell. This having been done, and the pot resealed, I ran whooping and laughing be-

hind the boy to harvest these frightful things from the sea.[1]
Hence, dear reader, has the color of my writing so suddenly
changed from somber black to richest purple—a sign, I hope,
of better things to come.

January 9, 1630

There has occurred a situation that has caused ill will between the boy and the Indians. Since I now have a good supply of ink from the slugs, this episode I will record as a warning to others who may trade among these tribes.

One morning, upon awakening from my rest among the
sandhills, I was struck at once by a terrible odor that suggested the presence of putrid flesh. The boy also remarked
upon this, believing it to be carried upon the breeze, and
shortly after we noticed a rising excitement among the
Indians.

The threat of cannibals seemed never far from the boy's
mind and almost at once he began his whining that we had
come upon a store of bodies and that a feast of human flesh
would no doubt follow. I could see no evidence for this idiocy
and told the boy so, once again declaring that had these Indians been eaters of men surely there had been opportunity
enough to gnaw our bones bare many times over. Furthermore, the living presence of Ela was opposed to his suspi-
cions, and at last we fell silent, still unable to discover what
the cause of the stink might be.

Throughout the morning the odor did not diminish,
rather it grew worse, and to our great amazement, with every
passing moment the excitement of the Indians increased—so
too did the rate of their travel, for instead of pausing here

1. Possibly a member of the *Holothuiidae* family, also known as sea slugs, sea
cucumbers, bêches-de-mer, or trepangs—Ed.

and there as was their usual manner, all speed was put on in what appeared a frantic rush to reach the source of the offense.

By noon we could see a great black mound upon the beach about half a mile distant. The Indians' pleasure was now ungovernable and many ran ahead, leaving the aged and infirm (indeed I had lately noticed several with thick fluxes running from the nostrils) to stumble after as best they could. The stench was unbearable, yet still we hurried on, and soon it became obvious that the thing upon the shore was the carcass of a mighty sea beast, its putrid flesh fouling the breeze.

From the Scriptures I had heard of Jonah's great fish that was large enough to swallow him whole, and now, before me, I surely saw its awful form with my own eyes. The length of the creature exceeded fifteen yards, its girth four yards, and the thick black hide, having burst from within by the swelling of rotted flesh, revealed a row of ribs whose cavity might contain a dozen Jonahs with ease.

About this mass the sky was white with sea birds, and upon the air hung flies so thick that to breathe openly meant the certainty of choking upon their vile bodies.

Yet, for all this, the Indians were overcome with joy. At first I presumed their excitement arose from the dreadful prospect of dining upon the creature's rotted remains, which fell away in maggoty lumps, but in this assumption, mercifully, I was wrong. Not one Indian went near the beast to gather flesh; rather, if any approached the carcass at all, this was done in the spirit of intense reverence, as though the monstrosity before them was nothing less than sacred.

These things made no sense to me and, indeed, Ela herself could offer me little enlightenment, having never seen such a thing in her time among the tribe. And so it fell to the boy, and his stupidity, to prove beyond doubt what I had so far only half-guessed.

Caught up on the excitement that prevailed, and ever eager to play the fool, he had been tumbling about the beach, as was his way. Then, alas, seeing his audience was otherwise distracted, and nothing daunted by the nauseating stink, he clambered through the rotting flesh to enter the carcass, where, hallooing and laughing, he called upon all to witness his internment within the ribbed belly of the monster itself.

At once an awful moaning went up from the throats of the Indians, some falling upon the sand, others turning to run, wailing, toward the dunes beyond. Nor in his rashness did the boy comprehend the disturbance he had caused. Taking the uproar to be sounds of encouragement, he began to caper about in the hideous offal, performing the actions of a caged ape until, quite exhausted, he looked about for approval.

None came. The Indians' dreadful cries had ceased, and now, in a more fearful silence, several warriors advanced toward him in attitudes of hate that could never be mistaken. Looking at me with utter despair, and finding no help, he ran, breathless, from the gaping jaws of the monster to throw himself into the sea.

Later, I could not discern that the Indians showed any direct malice toward the boy, but it is certain that the girl, Ela, was no longer as close to him as she was before. Though I tried to learn from her if this was her choice or a demand made upon her by the Indians of the tribe, I had little success. All the same, the fact that she ignored him had a profound effect upon the boy. He returned to his brooding, solitary ways, lingering behind the sled as we moved and complaining of illness and fevers, while never ceasing to fondle the ring that hangs about his neck.

January 19, 1630

Although I am now no great distance from the Shining Hills, I believe I will never enter them or learn their secrets. Again and again, the boy has brought me to the depths of despair, and I am obliged to record here such details of his actions, insofar as they have destroyed all hope of my future achievement in this land.

Having arrived at this camp some four days ago, I was pleased to see the closeness of the hills and therefore resolved once again to form a good impression upon the Indians so that I may procure a guide from among their number. I had hoped that this might be Ela, but alas, once more the boy has used his wiles to lure her under his spell and she has become lost to me. Together, these two disappear for hours upon end, and I begin to wonder that the tribe would allow such a young female these freedoms with a stranger.

For his part, the boy is no longer sullen, but his motives in associating with the girl I gravely doubt. Should he happen to spend time with me beside my fire, his talk is not of our future enterprise in trade, nor even our survival; all his thoughts are full of her and of how he might gain her favors. I will not record such things here, but he would lose no opportunity to possess her carnally, though I believe through simple ignorance she has no knowledge of his intentions and is innocent of similar desires.

However, these things are as they may be, and will no doubt run their course. My present concerns began when, through the boy's mismanagement of our goods, I lost the opportunity to turn mischance to good fortune.

Sitting about my fire not two days ago, I happened to hear a commotion in the camp and went to investigate. One of the warriors had by accident driven the sharpened barb of a spear into his forearm, whereupon it had broken off, leaving the needle-like tip embedded in the flesh. Females had made an incision to remove this, but to no avail, either because of the quantity of blood obscuring their vision or because the piece was too small to locate.

Believing that I could help, I ran to the pot in order to fetch the burning glass, by which means I might be able to magnify the offending particle and hence remove it. Yet, try as I might, I could not find the glass and noticed at once that not only were many of the wooden toys missing, but also that the limited supply of goods remaining had been packed from beneath with grass and leaves, in order to delude me into believing nothing had been removed.

I guessed who the thief would be: none other than the boy himself, for the Indians would never dare approach the pot nor indeed think of performing such subtle deception.

I was not able to locate the culprit until that evening, and then, having taken him off alone into the scattered forest trees, I set about abusing him for his wickedness, demanding that he confess to the theft and return the goods.

I have no words to express what now occurred, nor even to this day can I believe the sight that presented itself before me.

At first he heard my words with his usual sullen silence, then he raised his head, and with a boldness I had not encountered since his challenge to me at the dry riverbed, he stated that the goods had been given to the girl as tokens of his "love"—his word for anticipated sexual favors. However, to his fury, he found that these offerings had proved useless, for as was the way of her adopted people, the girl had distributed our goods among her female companions and thus they were lost forever.

I had hoped, at least, that what he had taken might have been traded among the old men or warriors and some good may have come from his actions. Fool that I was. And in that moment, beside myself with rage, I began to beat him with my fists.

Then occurred the most fearful thing. Hardly had two blows landed upon him than, showing a strength I had never dreamed he possessed, he thrust me back, causing me to fall to the ground, while he seemed to rise up before me, his face and hair aglow with light—and most remarkable of all, the ring exposed upon his chest shone likewise.[2]

I remember little more, such was my terror—and in a moment he was gone—but even as I write I cannot grasp that vision, and assume, having no explanation other than sorcery, that for a brief moment a peculiar beam of the moon worked this miracle of light upon him.

That night, for the first time since the death of the unfortunate pup, Lucky, the boy did not sleep in my company. I regretted the loss of a companion of my own race, yet refused to soften in my feelings toward him.

It was not until Ela appeared before me some days later that I even dared to think how any good thing might come from the evil events that had passed. I had been sitting watching the Indians' ministrations to the sick, of which there now appeared very many suffering the same feverish ailment as the boy, when quite suddenly I was overcome by the sensation of being observed, and lifting my head, saw Ela standing before me.

It was a rare thing for the girl to speak to me. But this time, she said my name, then, in my own tongue—a little she

2. The reference to "rising up" may reflect Loos's belief in sorcery. However, the quality of being "aglow with light," a manifestation Pelgrom is said to have exhibited on several occasions, is scientifically plausible. Recent studies of auras, coronas, and energy surrounds of people experiencing intense emotions are well documented, as is the practice of Kirlian photography of such phenomena—Ed.

had learned from the boy—she said the word "lovely" and held out her hand. At first I could not comprehend, but upon seeing what she offered, her message became only too clear.

Sparkling in her palm lay a jewel of marvelous beauty.

Never have I been privileged to see the crowns of kings or princes, nor yet the regalia of the Mighty Church, but this I know, the jewel before me would have shamed the glorious treasure of the Holy Father himself, and I trembled as she dropped it into my waiting hand.

The stone was perhaps three and a half inches long and nearly an inch wide. It was transparent as fine glass, although no glass could be cut like this, being delicately shaped to a point at either end and reflecting light from no less than six faces, each identical to the other.

As best I could, using my hands and broken English, I asked where the stone had been found, and, to my delight, she pointed to the shining hills. But when I signed that she should take me there, she laughed in a careless way, and having done her good deed, was suddenly gone.

I slept that night with the jewel in my hand, my dreams filled with its presence, and in the morning, determined now to succeed in my enterprise, I arose with fresh heart.

From the pot I removed the remaining toys; there were only three; and with these under my arm and the jewel in my hand, I set to serious trading.

From group to group I went about the camp, holding out first the jewel, then a toy, working its wires as I did so. Many looked at me with stupefaction, others laughed, but to my amazement some bid me wait, and on their return, produced from bags of woven grass, jewels of like appearance to the one I held forth. On each occasion I was overcome with wonder. How could it be that savages such as these, who possessed no homes, lands, crops, or animals—neither sailed in ships nor dwelt in cities—could own such treasures, yet hold them in so low esteem, or be so ignorant of their value, that they should be stored in nothing more than bags of grass?

But what followed is beyond belief. For indeed, not only did they refuse to trade these jewels, they followed me about the camp in growing numbers until, as I knelt before a hut, absorbed in the inspection of another jewel, the toys were taken from the ground behind me, and I saw them no more.

So it was I lost all goods of trade in my possession, leaving nothing save the white stockings—of which the savages remain terrified—my journal and ink, the iron pot (whose sealing brackets have long since vanished) and the wooden sled upon which it rests. All else, save for the jewel given me by the girl, has been destroyed or stolen.[3]

I know that any hope of trading among these savages is over; indeed my remaining among them has lost all purpose, and other than the awful truth that I cannot live without them, I should gladly quit their company now and forever.

I conclude this entry in utter remorse, for though it may appear I could suffer no more, the boy has dealt another blow. This day he returned after so long away, leering and swaggering, boasting that at last he has taken Ela to wife, and as proof of his conquest—or its price—the leather band at his throat no longer carries the ring.

This concludes the fifth installment of the Loos journal.

---

3. There can be little doubt that the "jewel" in Loos's possession (and those shown to him by the tribe) was in fact a quartz crystal, sacred to the Aborigines but of no monetary value—Ed.

Item 31

From the Hamelin Herald, *August 19, 1986*

Teenager Reprimanded for Mercy Dash

Hamelin, Tuesday. A 17-year-old youth charged with unlawful possession of a vehicle was formally reprimanded in the Shire Court yesterday.

Appearing before Magistrate Edwards was Nigel Kratzman, student, of the Midway Roadhouse complex.

Highway Patrol Officer David Andrews told the court he saw a pickup truck emerge from scrub in the vicinity of the abandoned Neuland Aboriginal Mission shortly after 7 P.M. As the vehicle had no headlights and appeared generally unroadworthy, it was flagged down for inspection. A passenger in the vehicle was a local Aboriginal identified as Charles Sunrise.

Speaking in his own defense, Kratzman claimed he was forced to use the vehicle in order to get Sunrise urgent medical attention.

He said that he and 16-year-old Steven Messenger, also of the Midway Roadhouse, had taken Sunrise to the Nicholson Range Aboriginal Reserve to retouch ancient tribal rock paintings. Kratzman had left Messenger and Sunrise alone for a few minutes while he explored the area, but returned to find Messenger gone and Sunrise lying injured against the wall of an overhanging gallery.

Constable Andrews said Kratzman's claims of Messenger's involvement in the outing and subsequent accident could not be verified. He said Mrs. Messenger had seen her son standing among low scrub behind the Roadhouse shortly after noon, and Messenger was at home when Andrews telephoned him twenty minutes after Kratzman's vehicle was detained.

In reprimanding the youth Magistrate Edwards said that, while he could appreciate Kratzman's intentions, his lack of driving experience and the unroadworthy condition of the vehicle might well have led to further serious injury. He noted that the mercy dash could in no way excuse the fact that Kratzman had driven the vehicle on a major highway before Sunrise was injured.

Kratzman also faced charges of driving an unroadworthy vehicle and driving without a license. He was placed on a six-week good-behavior bond and released into the care of his mother.

Charles Sunrise was admitted to the Hamelin Base Hospital with head injuries. His condition is critical.

Item 32

A note Kratzman pushed through my window with some magazines on Friday, August 22, 1986.

Messenger,

I gave back all these magazines because I don't want anything from you around me. I would tell you this to your face but I wouldn't be able to control myself. And also I would most likely puke if I saw you.

One more time you got out of trouble, Clean Boy. Only this time it was important. Did you even care that old Charlie was dead? No. Like you didn't even turn up in the court to speak up for me. So where the hell were you? I couldn't even prove you were in the machine that day. Now it's gone too. That's my luck to get a rookie cop, not Norman who would have let me off. Over a year of work and thinking about what I could make of that machine—all gone for what? I don't even know or understand.

I couldn't say what happened to poor old Charlie because I didn't see, and when I got there you were gone as well. I looked for you everywhere and Charlie might still be alive except for me wasting my time on you. Trust you to light out when there was trouble. How the hell you got back, I don't know, but now it's over and too late to care.

My mother is taking me down south. I am going to enroll in a tech school course in mechanics.

I am sorry I ever met you and I hope I don't meet anyone like you ever again in my life. You think you are better than everybody but you're not. You're like a thing that lies on its belly in a dark hole, just lying there watching and waiting.

You are a bastard and no friend.

NIGEL KRATZMAN

Item 33

From the Standard Weekend Edition,
Saturday/Sunday, August 23/24, 1986

A Murderer's Diary
The sixth and final installment of the
journal of Wouter Loos

This extract, translated by Professor Hans Freudenberg, is introduced by Hope Michaels, Director of the Western Australian Institute of Maritime Archaeology

I am very grateful to the *Standard* for allowing me to introduce this final installment of Wouter Loos's journal and also to make a further public appeal for the recovery of the golden ring so often referred to in his writing.

Recently I have been rereading the articles with which Professor Freudenberg introduced the first and second sections of the journal and I must say his comments on the *humanity* of Loos now prove only too true—for nowhere are those human qualities more evident than in these, his final words.

Here, at last, the wretched castaway is forced to face the hopelessness of his situation. The undated, erratic, and at times illogical nature of his writing is evidence enough of his awful suffering; we can only wonder what we might have felt, and done, under similar circumstances.

Yet, for me, the tale of Wouter Loos remains unfinished—irrespective of the words from his journal printed here today—until each item he placed in that iron pot over three hundred years ago is finally recovered and given to the world. I refer, of course, to the missing ring.

In recent weeks, the mummified hand discovered with the journal was transferred from the Maritime Institute in Perth to the South Australian State Conservation Center in Adelaide, where the beeswax attached to it was examined using a newly acquired Perkin-Elmer gas chromatograph.[1] These tests prove conclusively that fractures in the wax had been made as recently as six months ago and that impressions in its surface were consistent with those made by the band of a ring.

In consideration of this evidence there can be no doubt that a ring was on the mummified hand at the time of its discovery and subsequently broke away or was removed from its wax retainer.

With the authority of the Historic Shipwrecks Act (1976), Federal invesigators will now formalize inquiry and search proceedings among members of the public involved in the discovery of the pot and its contents last April.

We can only hope that these inquiries are successful so that all the evidence will be made public—and Wouter Loos's story may be fully told at last.

The following journal entries are undated. All were written in a disordered fashion on the reverse side of previously used pages.

In my hand is a mirror.[2] I stand on the cliff top and signal

---

1. An instrument used to analyze naturally-formed resins and gums—Ed.
2. Mention of a mirror here is curious. Previously Loos has stated all trade goods had been lost, or given away by Pelgrom. While it is possible that this item was recovered by Loos, the mirror references could be entirely fictitious—Ed.

toward the horizon, which is a disk or upturned plate or bowl. Low clouds blur the edges and all below seems part of the space above. Here I see vessels massed with souls floating or flying as if on air. Should they see me, I will go home.

I rest my head on the earth and place a mirror between my face and the sea. This is not myself. This is another's face. Flies hover at the gaping mouth. Open sores thicken the lips. Vile matter seeps from the hollow eyes. This is a stranger's face. Should I touch it, flesh falls.

I have seen a serpent make itself new, coiling in the dust, catching the dull, dead skin to peel it away. When this is done the new skin gleams in the sun and a fresh creature forms.

The sun strips skin from my body, yet I do not shine as the serpent, nor am I made over.

The boy is become new. He shines in his pride as the Blessed of Heaven, not the cursed who crawl in the dust.

Above the waters he flies as an eagle. In his sin the earth cannot contain him.

I have seen him with women. Alas for Ela. She does not know his ways. When his fit of passion is past then.

Once I saw my father hold up a new child before the sun. It was market day and the mother lay on cobblestones behind her stall. Around her were scattered the cheeses she had fallen among. In her pain the woman had torn a cheese with her fingers.

My father knelt beside her, raising her from the stones. She punched at his shoulders with her fists, not understanding his intention to help. I stood to one side watching.

Soon she did not struggle. Her skirt was thrown up.

When the head appeared she fell back with a great sigh, going soft, so the child came easy. On her thighs was bright blood.

My father held the child high for the woman to see. He held it before the sun. I saw blood on the mother and the child and running down my father's hands and arms, on his sleeves and coat.

A woman brought a dish of water. She carried it in the crook of her arm, and a cloth also. She rinsed the child to clean away the blood and wiped it until I saw the shining skin and wrinkled face, which was alive and new.

I have seen enough blood. I will not become new through blood but through words. I will use the words of this book to begin.

What could I say? In terror Ela came to me, her face bleeding from his blows. She did not consider herself, but rather begged me to remain with the tribe and minister to them. A great illness has come upon them. The camp is thick with bodies.

How they suffer and die with feverish wailing. They paint themselves white with clay, and roll in gray ashes.

What good am I? Where is the use in me? She turns to me, my Ela, and weeps. But even yet she wears the ring, his bright one that made him whole.

Each night he comes, calling softly about the camp, outside the firelight. None dare face him. The young men, the warriors, the graybeards—all live in terror of darkness, for he moves by moonlight, his dreadful body pale and crouching low. He is the sickness. He is the vile one who has brought them death.

No longer does he fly as the eagle bathed in light. No

longer does he shine as the serpent in the sun. Hear how he seeks his prey, roaming the wilderness, crying as a night beast.

I promised I would not sleep, that I would keep watch to protect her. Because of my weakness I did not. By the dying firelight, he came prowling. Even now I sense where he crept, where he paused before the hut and bent to call her, luring her to him.

Ah, my Ela, my lovely one. Why did you answer? It was not you he yearned for, not you he sought after, but the ring.

Did you speak when you left? Did you whisper, "I will lead him away?"

The sound of your screaming was dreadful. At first I saw only him, his whiteness, clear against the night. Then you, your hair. I threw myself upon him. I did not abandon you to die. I threw myself upon him, yet there seemed nothing to grasp, no substance, and he was gone. I swear he was not flesh.

In the hut you spoke to yourself, you said, "Harry," over and over again. I knelt by you. I did not leave, you must know that.

In the morning the women came, their faces streaked white with clay, their voices wailing. In my own tongue, I said, "She is not killed. She is sleeping. Ela is not killed." They could not understand.

They covered the ring in dark gum. They wrapped the body in sweet smelling leaves. They raised her high above the earth, hidden in the branches, in the sky.

My hand falters. I ask, Who will read this? Who will believe? This record will condemn, in this world, or some other. How he lives I cannot tell, his habitation is unknown.

For myself, these things that remain I will store away.[3]

To the North my mountains shine. I am done with words.

So concludes the journal of Wouter Loos.

Item 34

Messenger, Midway Roadhouse

Dear Dr. Michaels,   August 29, 1986

I have been doing some straightening up in my room. Re-arranging things, etc. I thought I would send you all the articles I collected about my discoveries (and a little more). They might put your mind at rest. Then again they might not.

Everything is in order and numbered, just like history is supposed to be. But I don't need any of it anymore, because what I am keeping is my own piece of history, or dream package. It depends on how you want to interpret that.

I included the note from Kratz so you could tell what sort of person he was, that it wasn't just my say-so.

The business about losing the truck was his own fault. He could have said no at the start; he had the chance, and

---

3. What exactly were these things Loos stored in the pot? Researchers have assumed them to be the journal and Ela's mummified hand, no doubt presented to him by the Aborigines as a ceremonial charm—and still bearing the ring that Pelgrom had failed to tear from her even as she died.

However, months must have elapsed between the murder of Ela and the presentation of the hand, allowing time for the mummification process. What other things might Loos have gathered? What became of the white stockings and the well of ink? Possibly the ring was not the only object that vanished from that pot in the early hours of Sunday, April 13, 1986—Ed.

besides, he deliberately drove it down the mission the time he traded for the new seat. That had nothing to do with me. He made me sit on broken springs. He did it for that Charlie's comfort.

Which is another point. What happened to "poor old Charlie," he deserved. From the beginning he was the one who invaded my privacy, going into my special place (which I had previously marked and he knew it) and spying on my room (which he admitted). Neither did I ask to go to the mission or up the ranges. All of that was his own request. Then he came at me with his hand and snapped the leather. If he was pushed by me and injured, you could only call that self-defense. I can't see my responsibility for that.

Anyway, he was a mission black, which is not a big deal. I couldn't find one clipping about it in the paper and wouldn't have known he was dead if Kratz hadn't said so in the note.

When Sergeant Norman came to talk to my mother, he never said Charlie was in hospital, let alone dead. Or if he did, she didn't mention it to me.

But it's stupid going on about all that. It's over. The ring is safe for now, and that's the main thing.

I say for now, because that other one, outside the window, has not really taken my point, following me up the headland and worse.

With all the goings on, I forgot about the Life Frame, still left on the ant nests. The other day I took the magnifying glass and went up to have a look. There was nothing. At least, no bones. The wire cage was still there where I left it, but not a thing else. I got right down and even with the glass I couldn't find a trace of a bone, let alone a skeleton.

That was when I heard the wheezing. Because of that I knew right away he was behind me. I had to get up anyway or I would have been eaten alive by the ants, but I didn't feel at all comfortable up there with him, being so far from our trailer, etc.

I still couldn't see his features clearly either. He stood against the sun. He is tall enough in build, although I get the feeling he is sick, very chesty, from the way he breathes. I said to him I was looking for bones, for an experiment, but he didn't make any attempt to answer. He only put his hand out, like before, as if I was supposed to give him something. I thought if he wanted the ring he could bug off, because I worked too hard for that.

Since then he has turned up a few times, and yesterday actually was in my room, even with the lock slipped. He had his hands on my dresser, touching things. I said "Get out" very firmly, but he took his time, as if this was his room and my things were his.

What was worse (when I looked for it later), the aerial rod was missing and I know exactly where I left it, right next to the funnel-web construction I mentioned before.

I also noticed my window wouldn't slide shut, which was not good. It is out of square, like it has been forced open. Kratz might have done it shoving all those magazines through, or it could be that was how the other one got in. Or it could even be the trailer itself, settling into the sand.

Anyway, I think I should get out of here and go.

I saw Kratz leave the other day, and his mother. They took the Greyhound south. The way things are I think I should do something the same, but head north, and hitch. (I might get picked up by my father.)

Up north I could wear the ring every day, on my hand, right out in the open. Then I would find out what we can really do.

STEVEN MESSENGER
Midway Roadhouse

Afterword

BY

HOPE MICHAELS

Steven Messenger's personal writings, and the relevance of the various articles he chose to include in the project book, have been meticulously examined by police and scientists involved in the case.

Obviously, much of what he wrote about himself and his peculiar circumstances following the initial cave discoveries could hardly stand up to rational analysis. There is every reason to believe (and this will be partially verified later) that the bulk of the boy's fantastic narrative is the outcome of a serious psychological condition, probably schizophrenia.

It is therefore not surprising that the information provided in the project book has proved of no use in the discovery of his present whereabouts.

However, Senior Sergeant Ronald Norman has continued with his investigations into the case, motivated mainly by his high personal regard for the unfortunate Charles Sunrise.

There can be no doubt that the most significant outcomes of Norman's inquiries have come about as a result of his meetings with the Murchison District Aboriginal Council, an important body of Tribal Elders, of which Sunrise was a distinguished member.

Norman initially approached the Council when he realized that Messenger's detailed description of the sinkhole cave art almost exactly matched that given by Nigel Kratzman during his court hearing in August. At that time, Kratzman's claims of his visit to the gallery remained unverified, as Sunrise failed to regain consciousness.

In the circumstances, Council Elders met with Norman and granted him permission to visit the gallery—in their company. Norman and Kratzman are believed to be the only non-Aboriginal persons to have witnessed this phenomenon.

Except, of course, for Steven Messenger. Judging from Norman's reports of the rock art, there is now little doubt that Messenger was in the company of Kratzman and Sunrise on that fateful day, but what happened there, and why, and how he managed to return to his home in the given time, remains a mystery.

However, more worthwhile outcomes followed. After further deliberation, the Council also informed Norman of the existence of certain non-Aboriginal skeletal remains on sacred ground in the Nicholson Range Reserve. The remains, said to be those of "the little crystal fella," had been well known to Aboriginal people for centuries, and the knowledge of their whereabouts passed down through Tribal Elders from generation to generation.

Although aware of the archaeological significance of these remains, Norman has agreed not to publicize further details of his discussions until granted permission by Tribal Elders.

It is to be hoped that the Aboriginal Council will see its way clear to allow a small party of scientists to investigate this remarkable reminder of our mortality.

Sergeant Norman has also been responsible for the

recovery of the rusted remains of the Life Frame and Messenger's "perfect artefact," the sharpened car radio aerial he had used to dispatch his specimen. Messenger expressly stated that this aerial rod was missing from his bedroom (Item 34) and implied that this object was removed by his clone visitor. Norman located the Life Frame and aerial among ant mounds, almost five hundred yards from the Messenger trailer home.

A chromed alloy belt buckle, reportedly similar to one worn by Messenger, was sifted from the sand among these same mounds. Neither the aerial nor the buckle bore evidence of fingerprints.

The missing ring was never found.

Before concluding, I present two further pieces of evidence that I suppose should be made known. As a scientist, a dealer in logic and facts, I find both of them professionally threatening, but in this curious tale, where so much has been made of the bizarre, they have their place.

The following are extracts from the proceedings in the Messenger inquiry conducted by the Hamelin Civic Court, December 2–3, 1986.

From the Testimony of Mrs. Irene Messenger
Age: 41 years
Occupation: Waitress

QUESTION: And you were woken quite regularly by your son's screaming?
ANSWER: No . . . well . . . yes . . . it depends on what you would call regularly.
QUESTION: Mrs. Messenger, how often, let us say, in an av-

erage week, were you woken by the boy's screams?

ANSWER: Probably about once or twice a week.

QUESTION: And no doubt you associate these dreams, or nightmares, with the boy's discovery of the somewhat grisly evidence in the iron pot?

ANSWER: What?

QUESTION: You believe your son's nightmares were caused by finding the mummified human hand?

ANSWER: Well . . . no. That never crossed my mind.

QUESTION: Mrs. Messenger, I suggest that these terrible nightmares, the screaming sessions which you say the boy experienced, were caused by the shock he underwent in finding that mutilated hand on the school biology field trip in April.

ANSWER: Yes. I know what you're saying. I can understand English. And the answer is No.

QUESTION: Very well. In your opinion, what did cause these nightmares?

ANSWER: He was sick. And what happened to his father. So far nobody has said one word about that. How I was left to bring that boy up by myself. I did my best to—

QUESTION: His father?

ANSWER: That's right. His father. Killed in a rig accident on the highway up north—January 6 this year—a good three months before all this hand business you're going on about.

From the testimony of Meryl McAlpine

Age: 27 years

Occupation: Transport driver

QUESTION: Ms. McAlpine, can you identify the said Steven Messenger from this photograph?

ANSWER: Sure. There's no doubt about it. That's the same guy.

QUESTION: You're certain?

ANSWER: Sure. Except when I seen him he wasn't dressed like that. He wasn't wearing school uniform.

QUESTION: Will you tell the inquiry how and when you came to see the boy?

ANSWER: Right at midnight on August thirty-first. I was pulling in to refuel at the Midway truck stop when I seen him. He was hitching near the motel sign. I thought he looked good—you know—like something out of a movie. Maybe twenty-two or twenty-three. Not sixteen. I can't believe he's sixteen.

QUESTION: Do you recall what he was wearing?

ANSWER: Sure. No trouble. He had a red T-shirt and white jeans. Tight.

QUESTION: You say he was hitching. Did you pick him up?

ANSWER: Jeez no. I might have. I pulled in and gassed up, but when I was getting out onto the highway I looked back and he was gone.

QUESTION: Could you tell which direction he was heading?

ANSWER: North. He had his thumb—

QUESTION: Yes. Ms. McAlpine, your testimony has been very helpful to this inquiry. We certainly don't doubt your word, but there remains a problem with dates. Will you restate exactly when this occurred?

ANSWER: Midnight, Sunday, August thirty-first.

QUESTION: Ms. McAlpine, the problem we have is that your sighting of the boy occurred three days after he was last seen at his home—which, in fact, is situated right next door to the truck stop. Do you understand?

ANSWER: Sure. Where was he for those three days? You got me there, but if you don't believe the dates I said, you can check the logbook in my rig. Or better still, check the register in that motel. The night I seen that guy, the motel sign was flashing NO VACANCY and I never saw that before, not at the Midway. No sir, I thought that was really strange.

Finally, and on a more personal note, it was recently my pleasure to interview "Nigel Kratzman"—that being the pseudonym he jokingly chose for himself when I told him of this publication. He is a fine-looking, mature young man, happy and successful in his present trade course in mechanics—and very proud of the gleaming pickup truck he pointed out as his own.

On the subject of Steven Messenger he would only say, "Maybe the Hitchhiker got him"—a reference, I believe, to a folktale well known in the Murchison District.

He was most unwilling to discuss the past. In consideration of his future, I could hardly blame him.

Hope Michaels
September 1988
Midway Roadhouse

About the Author

Gary Crew lives in Australia, where he lectures in creative writing at the Queensland University of Technology. He is the author of several books for young people, including *No Such Country*. *Strange Objects* won the prestigious 1991 prize for Children's Book of the Year: Older Readers in Australia. It is his first book to be published in the United States.